Laura Del-Rivo

Where is My Mask of an Honest Man?

Holland Park Press London

Published by Holland Park Press 2013

First Edition

A CIP catalogue record for this book is
available from The British Library.

ISBN 978-1-907320-39-2

Cover designed by Reactive Graphics

Printed and bound by CPI Group (UK) Ltd,
Croydon, CR0 4YY

www.hollandparkpress.co.uk

Where is my Mask of an Honest Man? is a powerful collection of short stories set in and around Notting Hill, London W11. Though the stories share a common setting, they deal with a wide variety of issues and range from stark realism to the surreal.

'Dark Angel', part 1 set in 1951 and part 2 in 1982, could be seen as the author's commentary on her debut novel *The Furnished Room,* filmed by Michael Winner. It covers similar ground but now seen through the prism of the author's wickedly evolved style.

This and a few other stories feature Joseph Kuhlman a 'hip descendant of a tribe of lying prophets and psychotic visionaries', who may know more about a murder with a ballpoint pen. Yet, in other stories, it's the perk of the reader to decide whether he is the patient or the doctor.

'J Krissman in the Park' deals with the travails of an ageing writer, contemplating his rejections while surrounded by happy families in a park.

'The Professor A Katz Memorial Evening' is a hilarious account of Elizabeth Woolacott, a large-boned, energetic woman, giving a talk to mathematicians.

The title story, the longest, is perhaps the most autobiographical. In it 78-year-old Joan Byker develops a severe crush on her 38-year-old landlord, Harry Brightling. Set in the present day, the story is again beautifully observed, and you feel you're there with Joan and Harry in the key scene on the roof of Vernon Crescent. Their conversations keep taking you by surprise.

Laura's skill in describing people and her gift for writing dialogue makes this a collection full of breathtakingly observations about life.

For Colin Wilson

CONTENTS

DARK ANGEL

Part 1 - 1951

Sunlight sliced the room into triangles. The visitation by brightness lasted 20 minutes, then the light deadened, returning the landlord's furniture to a solid state. The room enclosed the mind of its tenant Joseph Kuhlman.

His eyes, set close together, were the colour of holy oil or dirty engine oil; untrustworthy and fervent as a hip descendant of a tribe of lying prophets and psychotic visionaries.

He had bought his narrow black jeans from a shed whose location was passed by word of mouth.

Mr Angel's shed was on a bombsite in Tottenham Court Road. A group of three lock-ups with corrugated metal shutters was set back from the permanent businesses by an area of rubble and rat shit in process or reduction to mineral powder. AAAble was a purveyor of paraffin and not new furniture. There was a café, The Ideal. The three traders daily set out their goods and tables. AAAble especially displayed wardrobes and armchairs forming temporary domestic rooms on the disintegrating ground where atoms came and went.

In the sky it seemed that modern jazz riffed the location of American-style jeans to youth wanting to be cool.

Mr Angel was not permitted to hear the piano, wind instruments or hissing drums. He had bought the jeans because during the school half-term his son had come with him to the wholesaler's cigar smoke-filled cave under the arches of Liverpool Street station.

The same reflective London sky had shone on the substantial aesthetic of pigeon-hued masonry and the new insubstantial aesthetic which used the elliptical parabola of a flying saucer and the structure of an atom. The boy was undistinguished except that the irises of his eyes resembled cut and polished stones of turquoise.

'Buy the jeans, Dad. I can help carry them home.'

Mr Angel was defrocked middle class in striped suit and Homburg hat. His body was large and strong but inelastic; his fingers approached and prodded surfaces. He was cloudy and occluded, now unexpectedly popular with students who were respectful to him, speaking his name as if it was an honour and distinction because the new generation wanted to outfit itself from his trestle tables rocking on debris. Accordingly, Mr Angel moved his regular stock, of imperfect socks and ladies' vests in pink outside, to the back while he waited optimistically, being a man of much complexity, for ruin.

Joseph Kuhlman deduced that AAAble was the source of his landlord's furniture.

'He treats his tenants like cockroaches, he wants to stamp us into the ground, well I will stamp him into the worn-out carpet he has provided me; it has bald patches worn by the furniture of previous owners. Then I will lock him into a wardrobe.'

For this he would need the help of his girlfriend who was fat. Kuhlman was undernourished. His jackal hunger was not satisfied by blocks of corned beef in yellow, lacy fat, or fruit pies containing diced swede in syrup. Although thin, he was dangerous because of his disproportionate reactions and his experiments in anti-clockwise behaviour. To be thus analytical was to be sociopathic.

To go out, Kuhlman wore a hooded jacket, the narrow jeans, and socks made up of towelling. The winklepicker shoes stolen from a Berwick Street market stall had seemed sharp but a rainy day had proved them made of painted cardboard, the product of a desperate East European country. The humped hood and curl of legwear to pointed

12

toe gave a medieval prance and caper to his progress to the tube station.

Tanker had a pale moon face. Her skin was satin, her features peaked. Especially her left eyelid drooped; the eyelashes drowned downwards like the legs of insects. She was uneasy with the other girls in The Hole therefore if she ran with anyone, and because of her plumpness she ran slowly, she ran with the boys.

Kuhlman acknowledged her ability to make scenes with shop managers, ticket inspectors and others. He took the opportunity of confusion in shops to steal food.

She would already be waiting in The Hole because her subservience to him was a form of aggression.

Kuhlman's parents had doted on his intelligence. However, in The Hole there were others whose chess minds roamed higher strata of the atmosphere, or who were graduates of subjects in which cheating was impossible. For his part he had dishonesty and fervour. He made a lists of books to read.

The squalor of The Hole was peaceful. It gave absolution. The café was formed of two cellar rooms beneath unsafe stairs. Some habitués might not have been admitted elsewhere. Others exercised their preference for filth over the clean homes of their parents.

Kuhlman and Tanker sat thigh-to-thigh. Hers were the legs of Venus, plump-kneed with slender ankles.

He said, 'I'm going to kill the landlord when he goes to the furniture shop.'

'Oh, can I come too?'

Those gathered on chairs and benches were an electrical engineer, a railway porter, a typist, an art student, a hospital porter, a milkman and a teacher.

The teacher said, 'Excellent, comrade. Once the landlord is dead, the tenants can take possession of the house in the name of the workers' commune.'

13

'That isn't my idea,' Kuhlman explained. 'I want to be a holy man. I want revelation. But how can that happen in a room where sunlight visits 20 minutes of the afternoon, which is filled with cheap brown furniture and a dusty carpet?'

The etiquette of The Hole was that all were equal and taken at their word. Thus, one describing himself as deity or royalty was addressed as God or King without ado. For this reason, all assembled considered the predicament of Joseph Kuhlman.

The milkman was youthful with a downy chin. His boyish brow was bisected by a crease from squinting at doorsteps and equations.

'The timespan of sunlight is geometrically determined. There is therefore no profit in killing a landlord.'

The engineer, who stammered, suggested a system of mirrors which he offered to install in the interests of research.

The typist wore an antique velvet hat. She also wore a long tubular coat of black wool crepe. These curiosities might have come from a grandmother's trunk. She had presence, but said nothing.

The railway porter, a simple soul, mentioned that he had bought, with coupon and postal order, some rose petals dropped by St Teresa from heaven.

Kuhlman insisted, 'But the landlord has insulted me by renting me this hovel. I have been insulted.'

The hospital porter was a good-natured fellow, provincial in accent and clothing, who carried books in a shopping bag.

'I agree with Dennis,' he nodded to the railway porter, 'that the problem is religious. In your spiritual condition, you should read William James' *Varieties of Religious Experiences* or Heidegger's *Being and Time.*'

The intellectual starveling, the famished jackal Kuhlman, wrote each title onto his list. He had a sensation of imminence; of a breakthrough about to occur if he could force these books into his brain by the dog leg-shaped theft of borrowing without return. Transcendence was a pilfer away.

God pushed through the tables. He was a tramp. 'Buy us a tea.'

Mr Angel cogitated such subjects as ethics, business and digestion. Each lunchtime in particular in The Ideal Café, he pondered mutton chops whose rim of carbon-scented sizzling fat could be mashed into potatoes and gravy. Liver was cheaper. To eat liver would not ruin his business, or by progression, make homeless his son with the polished stone eyes. Unquiet in mind, he approached the counter, not knowing what words would be delivered, he sadly punned, from his mouth. 'I'll have the liver.'

Mr Angel's cousin from Manchester entered The Ideal. 'Henry! Let me buy you lunch.'

It was too late to change the order. 'The usual' had been confirmed.

Powdered coffee was spooned from a catering-size drum. Mr Angel now held a metal tray seemingly randomly, but actually by cause and effect, spotted with rust. On this, slightly unclean, tray was a bunch of cutlery and a thick white plate, also smeared, causing Mr Angel to wonder if the smear was on his own glasses or whether monochrome was a function or property of despair, because he had been tempted and then mocked. From the liver arose the odour of bile, of another animal's digestion, of pungent clay, like the Plasticine his son had once played with.

Later, he sat in his shed prodding into place a pile of knickers, peach, pink and eau de nil rayon bloomers to the knee.

His cousin told him of a family funeral to be held in Manchester. Mr Angel considered the proposition that he might recover the train fare by visiting the Manchester wholesale district. A small profit might even be made

15

unless the propriety of God, more dreadful than the propriety of Mr Angel himself, demanded a loss.

'Only for me, such perplexity. To others, it seems easy.'

The cousin said, 'Is this the new schmutter? People wear it? Who wears it? The Teddy Boys? Or like in France, the South Bank?'

The cellar rooms of The Hole were filled with argument and cigarette smoke. Whenever the door at the top of the stairs opened, cold slid in. Several people wore the ex-Naval duffel coats released through government auction in Plymouth. A beautiful art student who wore an historic coat with big collars and cuffs like a highwayman stood on a chair.

The evening's discussion centred on the international brotherhood of physicists, who in peacetime had lectured at each other's universities and had been as uncles to each other's children, which activities had been interrupted by the war. The best minds had been pressed by their governments into competing against each other to make possible a nuclear bomb.

Kuhlman was bored and thrilled as into the night the hospital porter expounded existentialism, the milkman logical positivism, the teacher dialectical materialism. There was also a discussion about who among them was in love with whom. God said, 'Give us a fag. What, you only got Woodbines?'

In a ferment, Kuhlman left the café. He held the talk to his breast like a vial. Occasionally, he stopped walking to sniff its elixir. He could not equate his persecution by the looming furniture of his landlord with the persecution of beautiful minds that were not Aryan, Marxist or in the service of finance. Neither was London a post-war zone occupied like the city which manufactured cardboard shoes. He did, however, believe himself the victim of injustice.

For the funeral Mr Angel wore the cashmere overcoat which had belonged to a deceased gentleman whose grieving, but fashionable, widow had demanded payment in clothing coupons. Mr Angel was in love with this overcoat because bespoke tailoring was the subject which he understood.

He locked his shed early in order to catch the train. On the area belonging to AAAble there reared up a mighty wardrobe with decorated shoulders like the epaulettes of an officer of Emperor or Czar. The gloved hand of such a marshal could signal a pogrom. Mr Angel therefore addressed the furniture, 'I am innocent.'

The wardrobe contained two gallon tins of paraffin which a customer was to collect.

Tanker said, 'Are you sure that's the landlord, not the tailor?'

'The tailor doesn't wear an overcoat and doesn't look at wardrobes to buy for his tenants. Besides, you can see his shed is shut. He's not there.'

Kuhlman felt invulnerable. His eyes were pinned open. A shift, or sleight, of aspect had replaced the group of three sheds with a replica group that was not boring. When he surveyed unblinkingly the overhead signboard AAAble, he saw a signboard that was identical, except that it was not boring. It was not interesting; it was null. Its existence could not affect him. He gazed dispassionately, as if from a commanding height. His peripheral vision noticed that a metal tray had been left or thrown out. The lights of a passing bus patterned it with winking eyes, but he did not need its complicity, as he did not doubt that to applause he would skilfully avoid treading on it. Nothing oppressed him. He could skate on thin ice, he could kill with impunity. He was the holy joker.

Had it been explained to him, in his exalted state, he would have respected the logic of a man protesting his innocence to a wardrobe. It had not been explained.

'You're not innocent, you louse, you bloodsucker, you rent me a room without light, I'll push you in the wardrobe.'

Kuhlman said to Tanker, 'Why are you so fat? You can't run away quick enough.'

A week later, a police constable crossed the unstable wasteland, the ballroom of electrons, occupied by the three sheds. Mr Angel could not explain how a wardrobe had become the field marshal of Emperor or Czar. He had pleaded, been arrested, falsely imprisoned and soused in paraffin. The overcoat which he loved was ruined. Full of grief, he described the weighty slime of cashmere, the precision of the lapels, the lining of satinised silk, the pockets of velveteen. Conclusively, the buttonholes on the cuffs undid and did up.

The policeman said, 'But who attacked you, sir?'

'You can't find such pre-war quality now. For example, my brother-in-law has a rag yard in Wapping. He has a Government licence to collect fabrics from bombed buildings. A machine compresses the rags into blocks, officially for mattress stuffing and blankets; can you trust not for overcoats? Life troubles and perplexes me, Officer, but I understood that overcoat and now I can never explain to my son, and God willing, his son, the thing that I understood. Customers require of me only American-style jeans and imperfect socks.'

'Now you mention it, in my job I need socks.'

'For you, I'll reduce the gents' half hose by sixpence.'

'And tell me who attacked you.'

Mr Angel must decide whether to protect his attempted murderer or to lose business during a trial. He retreated to the badger sett of his own complexity.

'I didn't see them. They probably escaped into Tottenham Court Road and down the tube station.' In business dread and anxiety he repented the sixpence taken from the socks.

The sociopath Kuhlman would not take the teacher as his mentor because he, Kuhlman, was uninterested in class struggle. The ethos of toleration within The Hole was in his favour but he was contemptuous of solidarity. The hospital porter had provided a philosophically sensational reading list but no osmosis pushed the books, stolen but unread, into Kuhlman's understanding.

'I shall write a novel. Its title will be *Dark Angel*.'

The hospital porter was himself working on a novel, as were several regulars of The Hole.

Kuhlman bought a notebook whose black end boards reminded him of the false shoes.

'I will show you the first chapter when it is done so you can help me.'

Kuhlman's next room was half a basement. The back half was occupied by an artisan, a maker of lampshades. Kuhlman and Tanker had the front room, below the pavement. The meter of the gas fire took shillings at the turn of a metal butterfly. Kuhlman, who bitterly believed that theft from an owner of property was revenge, therefore permitted, burgled its coin box, but the flicker up the friable incandescent brick was insufficient to heat the room. As in the previous room he was appalled by the intractability of matter when matter took the form of furniture. In paranoid, self-justifying manner, he paced the room screaming, 'Vile! Vile! Why is the wood varnished in treacle? I have the right to protest against such poverty and wretchedness.'

The lampshade maker, a Buddhist in his own right, was undisturbed by his noisy neighbours.

19

Kuhlman soon decided that Tanker was too stupid to be the companion of genius. An example of her stupidity was that while he was trying to write, she washed her jumper. She washed, rinsed and wrung the jumper in the little corner basin where they also washed up, prepared vegetables and made their toilettes. The cotton floral skirt of the basin curtained the shelf where they stored their little food.

Finally, she hung the sheep-smelling thing of wet wool over the wire guard of the fire and spread newspaper to absorb the drips.

Kuhlman awaited each drip. Then he threw off the blanket in which he had been hunched and went out to buy milk and soap. Because it was Sunday none of the shopkeepers would sell him soap. He was embittered by the stupidity of everything and by the smugness of shopkeepers who used the Sunday Trading Law purposely to thwart, frustrate and humiliate him. Finally, he descended into an underground public lavatory, where he stole a bar of soap, also public, that smelt of gardenias.

On the way home he noticed that the corner grocery which he had first tried was now closed. He kicked the door, making a crack shaped like a river delta.

'I am Kuhlman, criminal of the gas meter, thief and murderer. Now regret not selling me soap.'

When he entered the basement, Tanker was cooing childishly to the douce maker of lampshades.

Kuhlman put the pint bottle of milk on the table and went out again. He rode the Piccadilly Line to Hounslow West from where he walked to the roundabout of the A30. The ex-hospital porter, having received an advance from a publisher, had given up his job and moved to Cornwall. Kuhlman would hitch-hike there. His pocket contained a publicly owned bar of gardenia soap. He was a dangerous literary jackal.

Only when running for the lorry that had stopped for him, he realised he had left behind the black notebook.

Part 2 - 1981

The arterial Ladbroke Grove had an edgy charge of sirens and danger; confluent Portobello was raffish; however the criminal and arts cultures were outweighed by pedestrians with shopping bags. Psychopathy was barely sufficient currency to squat a room in a house iced with stucco. The basement had been filled in with breeze blocks. All the other rooms were squatted.

Kuhlman was now a figure of barefoot messianic shabbiness, trailing a coat which had belonged, after the camel, to a man richer and less emaciated than himself. His sandals of desert pilgrimage had been cut from rubber tyres. He inappropriately released nervous energy in rapid blinking or facial spasms. These tics did not occur when he was focused, for example, on painting his room white.

He scratched his arms. 'Fair is fair. I pay no rent, but I seem to be a hostel for unwanted insects.'

He formed the custom of going out early to walk through the market. The traders in fruit and vegetables, whom he defined as autonomous, used their freedom to impose on themselves rules and habits, one of which was to arrive between the shafts of iron-wheeled barrows before shops opened. On days of national significance, each absolute governor of a pitch demarked by white painted lines hung from his or her barrow the flag of St George.

The arriviste, not hereditary traders in other goods, did not hit the kerb until about 8am, when they threw from their vans sacks, plywood, metal struts, clothes hangers, dirty plastic sheeting, stepladder, mirrors, which took an average one and a half hours to assemble into a business.

On one such expedition, Kuhlman heard a woman screeching. She had been fat with mousey hair. She was now a skinny bleached blonde with amphetamine eyes like flies. She wore leggings of ice blue, stretch fabric threaded with lurex and a brief jacket of flossy pink fibres

21

of synthetic monkey hair. She was viciously struggling in the doorway of the supermarket with a security guard who was attempting to search her bag.

'Take your hands off me, fucking rapist perv!'

Kuhlman thought that she had been his woman but was uncertain which one. He told the guard: 'I work for the BBC. Is this how our viewers will see you treat your customers?'

Tanker ran instantly, but as before, slowly. He caught up with her round the corner, where she clung like a butterfly to a dirty wall. The man now with her, of the mixed race generally described as black, was of an age to be her son but was probably her lover.

Kuhlman asked the man, 'Where's the place?'

'You could try the Golden Cross.'

'Thanks, man. We'll see you there later.'

The man said, 'Laters, Marian.'

'Laters, Shane.'

Leaving with her, Kuhlman asked, 'Is Marian your name?'

'Sometimes. I've got to get my gear.'

'Where's your gear?'

'All over.'

Kuhlman quickly understood that she was one of a tribe of white women to whom the streets were a hotel: gypsies with the rights to a bathroom in one place, a bed or a cupboard in another. At one address, a Guyanese man equably handed over a bag and a jumper. At another, a Scottish redhead said, 'I know you've got my fucking bra, you're fucking wearing it.'

'I want my Ribena and my clean knickers, fucking ginger skank.' She said to Kuhlman, 'Do you really work for TV or was it a blag?'

'A blag. Where now?'

'Shane lives with his mum. She lets me stay in his room.'

Near St Charles hospital, they entered a row of new council houses, each with a small garden. In a steamy kitchen, a statuesque Irishwoman with badger-colour hair was filling in a magazine quiz. Under her shawl she wore a man's navy tracksuit with the logo of a sports brand.

Tanker said, 'I've got you some stewing steak, babes. Do you need cigarettes?'

Shane's mother said, 'Oh, stewing steak. Thank you, Marian. No, I've got cigarettes. Are you going upstairs?'

'Yes. This is Kuhlman.'

'Will you make him some tea?'

Shane's bedroom smelt of cannabis and laundered polyester. A football poster was over a single bed.

Tanker's lurex threaded leggings were soiled with grey frost at the knees. She looked rough in shoplifted chic. She smelt of a perfume oil she said was patchouli.

He said, 'Did we live in a basement?'

'Where we lived?'

'Yes. I was writing in a black notebook.'

'Not much writing. Plenty of talk.'

'What happened to my black notebook?'

'I expect you took it with you when you fucked off without telling me. Got any skins?'

She had a manner of tripping over words in a spoken scribble. She was itchy; she picked at herself. Recognition of the discomforts of use altered and made easy the footing on which they stood.

He said, 'No, I didn't take it to Cornwall. Where is it?'

'I don't know.'

'Yes you do.'

'A boy came. Or I could ask Shane's mum.'

'What boy?'

'I don't know how old boys are. Eight. Thirteen. He had beautiful turquoise eyes. He said you'd sent him.'

'Did you believe him?'

'Not especially. I'm taking your last ones.'

23

'Did you give him my book?'

'Probably. Don't keep asking me things. You sound like a white man.'

He noticed that this remark was witty. It contained three pieces of information; that she now preferred black men; that she would consider him an honorary black man; and that this privilege was contingent.

He said, 'So you never saw my book again?'

'Yes! I did! The book was pushed through the letterbox soaked in paraffin. The boy was trying to set us on fire, babes. The lampshade man kicked the book into the area. Two fire engines came but the fire was out by then.'

The holy prophet Kuhlman knew that his book of fervent second-hand philosophy was sufficient to burn a house and rejoiced.

'Have you got any money, Kuhlman? We need a bottle of Blue Nun and some cocaine.'

'We'll go to the Golden Cross.'

On the way, he recited the fame of the hospital porter, now a philosopher; the engineer, now a physicist; the girl in her grandmother's clothes, now a novel writer.

'Of everybody in The Hole, I haven't had satisfaction. Paranoid, oil-stinking, jackal-pissing Kuhlman with no satisfaction. I've suffered, I've made other people suffer, to get this bird to alight on me.'

'What bird?'

'The bird that alights on people but only shits on me. Can't you see, I'm covered in bird shit?'

'You're mad, Kuhlman. What's it called, this bird?'

'It's called grace, or genius, or transcendence, or revelation.'

He was in possession of a woman who seemed friends with, or tolerated by, all the black men outside the betting shop.

On Saturdays, the market had legendary or mythical properties. Costumes in shop windows and on passing girls streamed together to the effect that leopards and zebras, also pink monkeys, were cantering in fluorescent colours through the crowds.

The shop Angels was signed by a neon angel.

Mr Angel's son Morris was adequately, but not exceptionally, handsome and thickening, but not remarkably so, at the waist. His eyes resembled pebbles of semi-valuable turquoise. Angels sold clothes and accessories, such as T-shirts and leg warmers, which were on the breaking, or current, news of fashion and of a quality somewhat above trash. Dayglo price placards razzmatazzed bargains which were not so cheap as to downgrade the articles to those of copyists further down the chain.

Moderately hard geezer Morris Angel was famous for a gangster revenge act involving arson; for establishing that the rag trade belonged not to old men with cigars but to the young; for being the first of his contemporaries to wield a brick-shaped car phone; and for the slogan: 'New stock every hour'.

Morris Angel did not recognise Tanker from the past, but monitored the fiftyish, skinny blonde because he distrusted her noisy insistence that she had paid for her pink monkey jacket. He had discussed with the staff banning her; but she sometimes lurched against the rails, hooking up glittery things for which she paid with fistfuls of shakily held notes.

'Here babes; all this.'

Mr Henry Angel faltered into his son's shop and was held in a crossfire of acoustics and lights.

'Is that the firing squad? I am innocent.'

'Of course you are, Dad. Come into my office. I'll send out for coffee and gateaux.'

Mr Angel was to be driven to the house of his son and daughter-in-law to see his grandson. Absolute love had been born in Mr Angel the moment he had beheld the newborn; squinting, scalded by the birth process, sprawled like an amphibian on the beach of life.

Thereafter, Mr Angel was allowed to visit once a fortnight. Whenever he held his adored grandson, the infant bawled. Mr Angel lamented the skill of being which others found so easy. Even a baby sensed his disqualification.

'I wander in the wilderness. For my grandson, my darling little fellow, I should open a Post Office Savings Account.'

The white cube room was now inhabited by Tanker, Kuhlman and the insects which infested and bit his arms. His tolerance of these real or imaginary parasites was Franciscan. All life forms, all pestilences except humans, had rights. He refused, however, to own any furniture to come between him and enlightenment.

'Joke, ha, ha. How will I know if I am enlightened?'

'Well I won't sleep on any floor, babes, unless it has a carpet. I'm off to Shane's.'

Kuhlman had described the market traders in the manner of generalisation, like a writer of fiction. He had ascribed to them the motto: 'My barrow, my rules', together with patriotism. If, however, each statement was tested mathematically or linguistically, for its bare truth, the observation would be reduced to: 'On at least one occasion, during the period of any observation, at least one barrow displayed a piece of white polycotton bearing a motif which was possibly, when not distorted by the wind, a red cross.'

If the observation was magnified, the colour red would be describable as a wavelength, which he looked up in his Penguin Dictionary of Physics: 740-620 nanometres. At this degree of magnification, the context of flag and barrow would dissolve into confusion. The anti-confusion trick was to adjust the magnification to the level at which buying and selling, favourite TV programmes, timetables and politics came into the focus best suited to the human brain. For the convenience, protection and propagation of humanity the view of the multiverse must disperse to give value and importance to the opening hours of a supermarket.

He worked out that we inhabit a fold, or pocket, of limited information, with eyesight for use and pleasure, but with that sight protected from bombardment by electrons and galaxies. The past could be remembered, but not the future. Some people therefore experienced unease. The confidence trick that sustained their existence was nevertheless a confidence trick. Joseph Kuhlman was not the only paranoiac.

The patchouli oil which Tanker used reminded him of a carnivorous plant in the greenhouse at Kew. The plant had been labelled, explaining the rarity of its flowering and that its putrid smell attracted corpse-feeding insects. The smell of patchouli was not, of course, the smell of putrescence. What the two smells had in common was that they glued themselves to touch. Already, his fingers and clothes were contaminated with patchouli. Tanker said it was an essential oil sold by Indian stalls on the market.

'Do any of them sell black notebooks? I've had some interesting ideas. I believe I can prove I'm not paranoid. A conspiracy exists to make us believe the world is real.'

It being Saturday, many fashion stalls were out. Some traders used mannequins. Egg shapes of polystyrene granules wore woolly hats. The legs for tights display were expensive because rounded; but torsos, being shield shapes that stacked flat, were cheap. Kuhlman did not examine his own actions as good or bad, but as events to be licked, sniffed and tasted. A quality of plastic was lack of quality, specifically smell, to prove which he sniffed the underside of a female torso, wearing a lace camisole, that swung from a butcher's hook, and found no Tinkerbelle urine scent, no fish, no rectal B vitamin.

Years ago, he had not understood the books appropriated from the hospital porter, getting only as far as the opening chapter of *The Varieties of Religious Experience*. The narrative was simple and, in the original, had beauty. The subject Fox had been told by God to walk barefoot through the market place, crying, 'Woe to the bloody city of Lichfield.'

A market with its co-ordinates permitted and not permitted sheltered the weak-minded and the mad: employed the unemployable. Kuhlman himself had shed the coat of punctured bald camel to earn hand-outs for pushing barrows and carrying shoeboxes to a van. Had not his inspiration about multiple realities and the turning of reality up and down, which made everything more interesting, started from a football flag on a barrow?

Tanker, with her soliciting eyelid and now grubby pink monkey-hair, beckoned him from a stationery stall.

'Look Kuhlman, here babes, black notebooks.' She was snatching at and disarranging the books to cause confusion favourable to theft.

To sustain his shaky employability, however, Kuhlman raked his pockets for coins while snorting the cover of the book he had chosen. As before, a property of plastic was lack of property but he inhaled the potential for heat and combustion which was implicit in its matrix oil.

The trader recognised him as helping on a shoe stall and gave him a discount.

'Inflammatory,' Kuhlman explained. 'I will write something inflammatory.'

The academic who was to open the Professor A. Katz Memorial Evening wore her best dress. Elizabeth Woolacott was a large-boned, energetic woman. The dress, from an Oxfam shop, was antique gold velvet in sumptuous folds of burnish and tarnish.

Before the start of proceedings she hurried to the ladies' lavatory. She was holding her notes and a glass half full of white wine. She placed both objects on the ledge over the washbasins, entered a compartment and hiked up the dress, showing a bush of black, wiry pubic hair. She pissed, wiped and pulled the chain. The dress fell back to mid-calf.

She abandoned the wineglass, retrieved the notes and made her way to the lecture hall, whooping in mezzo-soprano to a colleague.

On the dais, through habit, she looked for the blackboard of equations.

— Ladies and Gentlemen.

She spoke bracingly of the mathematical papers which bore the late Professor's name and indulgently of his putting on terrorist airs to the National Security Agency.

— The mischief of an old man.

The body of Professor Katz was under the flint- and chalk-bearing earth but his phantom body had a phantom erection caused by sexual shock. He was transfixed by the suddenness of Elizabeth Woolacott's pubic hair as he learned that the Lecturer in Modern History and Administrator of Studies did not wear, and presumably during the years of their sharing the Uni Common Room had not worn, knickers.

Katz had died in quite good conditions although some of his underground neighbours had died as semi-transparencies surrounding the imbecilic O through which

29

gruel was spooned. The last air now squeezed from his lungs in a groan of desire for chestnut purée, café conversation, chess with the Agent of the National Security Agency and the lifted skirts of women.

Seemingly a procession of implacable women bore down on him: office worker, traffic warden, receptionist, primary school teacher: all straitly bodiced but naked from waist to knee socks.

— Help, help.

Numbers and women had been his dominatrixes. The numbers on taxis and receipts had demanded their prime or non-prime status. Decimals and the needs of women had infinitely recurred. Each had nagged to be Fibonacci or bought shoes and washing machines.

— Elizabeth, if you say your wineglass is half full we must quarrel, because the ratio of original wine to wine drunk is 1:½ (the square root of 5 + 1). But you are stronger than me; jolly and sporty, so I must surrender.

He had been in bondage to two strict mistresses; two cruel governesses.

— We numbers are more important than your wife's (that bitch's) dinner.

— Your dinner is ruined. Even now you're dead you can only get it up for voyeurism and fantasy.

They could wrangle over his grave as he had wrestled with the Agent over the chessboard. As anarchist and chess player he was too old to threaten the commerce and military which the Agent was employed to patrol. He was 81, not 18 in his prime with foreign labels on his underwear.

Sensibly, she had drunk only half a glass of wine before her speech. While the others had the platform, she sneaked to the bar-buffet for Chablis and canapés of smoked salmon and cream cheese. If she ate now, she would not have to cook at home.

— Jolly yum.

30

Professor Katz was probably married and of course too old, but she had always been a bit keen on him and had bought the dress of gilded silk velvet in his honour.

— What have I, Katz, ever done but play the fool on the edge of infinity?

J Krissman in the Park

His outfit was not absurd on an old man in midwinter: knitted ski cap, second-hand coat of good quality and bright white trainers. Privately, to conserve warmth, he was bandaged in a winding sheet of thermal underwear and tubular medical crepe. The frail knees were anointed with menthol.

J. Krissman, the name with which he signed his unpublishable writings, experienced his body as an immediate area of seepage and discomfort. His organs however persisted with their functions, such as the filtering of his urine; the skin shed its comet dust of dead cells. Also the skeleton, the specific diagram in bone laced with dainty capillaries, advanced him through the black, green and copper-tinted urban park.

The winter light made the trees distinct. Pollarded branches ended in bristling knuckles. High in the tallest tree, a slovenly heap of dead vegetation was unmoved by the wind. Krissman considered whether it was possible to quantify in terms of physics the stillness of the squirrels' dray which seemed in a different dimension from the tonnage of surging air. He remembered that the purpose of his walk was to purify a letter.

His mouth contained the protein odour of the digestion of dead plants and animals; and words.

'I read your article in the New Scientist on Multiverse Theory describing two hypothetical Universes, one predicated on a cold Big Bang and the other lacking the Weak Nuclear Force. I need to ask, is there a law which states that if a Universe can exist, it must exist?'

As he spoke, he experienced agitation and wonder, as if winged archangels had sprung up at his shoulders.

'That is, is the hypothetically possible the same as the necessary?'

33

Due to the opaque property of matter to the handicapped human eye, the remaining body of Krissman showed no immodesty of skull or bone, no unseemly lolling of lights and liver. He leaked only mild warmth, which activated the volatile film of menthol. However, he was in a rage and pain because in old age his mind as well as his body was becoming uninhabitable. The cause of such turmoil was that he hated humanity, its mass and mediocrity. The hatred had set up camp in his mind and its angry and unpleasant manoeuvres without cessation gave him no rest. He chose the park for his daily walk to avoid as much as possible the pinkish mass of foolish faces.

Among J. Krissman's rejected writings, The Animal Not Solipsist But Creative proposed that meaningful existence depended on its being verified and recorded by a life form conscious of being conscious. The author argued that knowledge is secondary creation; thus the dinosaurs were retrospectively brought into full existence. Their terrifying reptilian roar would have been silent without ears. However, by this argument, his own unpublished work did not exist.

It seemed clear to him that for serious purpose, humanity was overproduced. Its billions were unnecessary; it was devalued by quantity. He wished it no harm but refused the imperative to love the massed pinkness, which was unlovable. In crowds, the unlovable became the hated.

Sometimes he felt as if wolves were eating his mind, but he did not know whether the wolves were other people or generated by himself.

For these reasons, it was necessary for his safety to bandage also his mind, which was more obscene than the stained and discoloured rags of flesh.

Me Oh Lord You have made to hate. I am even vain of my hatred, believing I am Your chosen hater. By anomaly I am an atheist and supporter of most liberal causes.

The pollarded branches clubbed the sky. The squirrels' dray was undisturbed.

The most dangerous was that the hatred was spreading from his mind to his soul and narrowing his ability to experience wonder.

A family group occupied a bench. Surrounding them like a gilded bubble was the superpower of the commonplace. Of the two young women, one held a pram containing a baby while a boy of about four clung to the pram handle. A youth, possibly the women's brother, who accompanied them, shared their sacramental Tesco biscuits.

This family represented the social class, which Krissman most feared and hated, that proliferated in Council estates.

The cold made him nauseous. His hands were plagued by black tokens; he pressed one subcutaneously bleeding hand over his liver which seemed swollen in its caul. The containment of such hatred was feverishly painful to Krissman. Being rational by type, he tried to analyse his hatred; that is, he tried to hold down and analyse the thing that was painful while the pain was most severe. It was revealed to him that he suffered from frustration of the will: that he willed these people not to exist but they did exist.

He was persecuted by their existence.

The wind dragged shapes through the grass around their bench; their wrappings of biscuits and crisps were also blown.

He dared not speak his thoughts aloud, 'You are unnecessary and therefore vile. Your love is complacent.'

The virtue of the young women was that they were ordinary and loving. The power of the ordinary overwhelmed that of the wretched Krissman. The quite pretty sisters hardly noticed him; then fluently dissed him, 'Ohmygod, how spazz was that?'

Nothing had happened except that an old man had passed a family in a park. The space between buildings was not even a park; only a public garden with trees, squirrels and benches. At the gate, Krissman turned his mind to the article which had described the other two viable universes. There would be few or no visible stars. He was too uneducated in physics and maths to expand his mind but the effort of trying to do so for several seconds expanded his soul.

People said that Kuhlman had killed the old priest. This was false. Kuhlman was a murderer but the crime had happened long ago.

The Boy on the Bike

Kuhlman was 11 when the war ended, and a black marketeer. He cycled to and from the USAF base where the Yanks took him up as a bright kid. He dealt in Lucky Strike cigarettes, Hershey chocolate bars, canned foods, nylons and other things. He came from a loving family but cultivated the qualities, independent and manipulative, which are traits of institutions. He could instantly turn vicious. In appearance he was an ancient child, cool but fucked.

He was 15 when he committed his definitive crime.

The Young Killer

There are vigilantes who attack strangers on the street. Such an enforcer is orthodox, he is enraged by any deviant styles which he believes himself commissioned to punish. The hip self-contained deviance of the puny boy, Kuhlman, insulted such a bigot who was pumped up with rightness.

It is generally supposed that death in street fights is not intentional. It is supposed, that is, that there is no moment to stop, to choose, or to decide whether one enemy should be irrevocably a murderer and the other dead. The irrevocable occurs during inattention. This was not Kuhlman's experience. He noticed that time slows in crisis. He therefore had time to choose whether to take murder into his soul. His choice was ignorant, but his own.

He killed using what he later named a ballpoint pen, but was actually a propelling pencil.

A Mild Man

When they met, Kuhlman was middle-aged but by anomaly looked younger because he had been laid waste but not fattened. He sometimes claimed to be a doctor. Father Quinlan was 93 and known as a saintly simpleton. His small bent figure shuffled down the market street in penitential shoes without socks. Even in winter he slept on the floor of the unheated presbytery.

Burglars broke in. Father Quinlan refused to identify or testify against them. He humbly explained, 'I have no property. Anything I seem to own is only borrowed from the common stock. There is nothing that is temporarily in my care that is worth anyone spending even one hour in a prison cell.'

The burglars returned and this time struck down the priest. Father Quinlan said, 'Poor fellows, they must have been desperate. I wish I had something to give them.'

He could be retiring to a Catholic nursing home. On the other hand his Christ-like reasoning would not necessarily be diagnosed as that of a straying mind.

Father Quinlan suggested, also humbly, that he give shelter to a lodger, a doctor, a possible convert, who surprisingly could tolerate the unheated presbytery.

Kuhlman and His Woman

Observing that his lodger, newly arrived on the doorstep, was being screamed at by a skinny blonde with eyes like flies, Father Quinlan asked, 'Will the lady also come in?'

Kuhlman said, 'No, the lady will not come in.'

Father Quinlan had a tremor of nodding, thus shyly observing his protector, or refugee, up and down.

Kuhlman was of medium height, and slim. His eyes, which were close set, burned like wicks in dirty oil and with an effect untrustworthy and fervent. His T-shirt and jeans were quite grubby. He also wore a sharp leather jacket that had seen action.

The woman said, 'Kuhlman, you shit, you're a fucking shit.' Then she lurched away on high heels.

Kuhlman told the priest, with an honest expression, 'I am a disciple of truth.'

Father Quinlan did not consider he had a right to be satisfied or not satisfied with this definition. He courteously showed Kuhlman to a room where he sheltered for as long as needed.

A Cold House

The presbytery was an extension, or outbuilding, reached by a passage. Inside, the almost empty rooms stored time-travelling parochial junk.

In his room Kuhlman did not sleep at night but sat up because he was listening wide-eyed. He was terribly cold, but the cold was an allowed-for condition; a metronome of awareness of cold. He wore all his clothes under the hipster jacket and was also wrapped up in the pink cashmere peignoir of his ex-companion. It had turned up rolled between a jumper and a towel in his backpack. Thus it happened that the third time burglars came, they were confronted by an androgynous psychopath who leapt the stairs wearing a marabou-trimmed gown and brandishing a grapnel.

They were routed by that quality of proportionality that was absent in Kuhlman; routed, that is, by a negative, a lack, a blank. Fortunately they escaped just in time so there were no bloodstains to explain to innocent Father Quinlan.

Next morning Kuhlman told the priest he would be briefly away. Like the shoes of the wandering Jew Kuhlman claimed to have left stuff all over the world. He travelled to Cornwall and retrieved his toolbox from the cottage of one of his more mediocre pilgrimages. He avoided a sensitive woman and the local shops where he owed money.

On his return, he worked to secure the presbytery windows and doors. For this he required a return payment that was not material.

Waiting

Father Quinlan had the mild palsy of old age. Kuhlman also showed spasms; a series of sniffs and blinks between voluntary and involuntary. The mind of Kuhlman was so concentrated that he achieved perfect stillness possibly by this commentary of unease.

Father Quinlan did not remark on this motor neurone displacement of his lodger except to say, 'The poor man is not at peace.' He waited patiently for Kuhlman to explain what he wanted that could be provided, such as joining in prayers.

Kuhlman said, 'That's not enough.'

The Squirrel

Father Quinlan stood by the landing window. The old man's face seemed composed of sickle moons and his hair, which had once been ginger, lay over his scalp in strands of white stained with mustard.

Kuhlman stood nearby, spiteful because he did not know if the priest was senile or transcendental. He had hoped that Father Quinlan saw revelation beyond the window but the old man was observing a squirrel in the bare tree that was trapped in milky light.

Father Quinlan said, 'Your squirrel can do no wrong. I do believe in the right of animals; what is your opinion?'

'When is an animal not an animal? May I de-worm my dog?'

Father Quinlan's sweet smile showed he was in a state of grace; not that he recognised complexity. He was holy, not clever. He made babyish coos as he did when reciting the rosary.

Was there nothing more than the oxygen deprivation caused by such praying? Kuhlman was not the man to be trifled with or fooled.

The Bargain

For days and nights Kuhlman was frozen by cold and also like a hunting animal. In the feverish reaches of boredom, he waited for Father Quinlan as he had waited for the burglars or, in his previous life, he had listened and attended to the speeded-up metronome of waiting for a coke dealer. He was convinced that supernatural experience existed and that Father Quinlan, with his simple smile and faraway expression, had got through. If he, Kuhlman, could equally endure in this tundra of boredom where even the subsoil was frozen, wouldn't Father Quinlan acknowledge his rights?

Meanwhile Father Quinlan prayed for Kuhlman's conversion without understanding that sensation was Kuhlman's morality. Only temporarily it was religious sensation.

Kuhlman Protects the Priest

Then Kuhlman's nightmares began. In the nightmares he had killed someone, sometimes it was an infant or a woman but always it was really Father Quinlan. He had pressed the

41

old man's frail skull between the heels of his hands to force out the truth. As a boy he had got away with murder but this time he was a suspect and DNA would convict him. While the footsteps of his hunters approached he regretted the waste of imprisoning someone quite intelligent and occupied in research like himself. He had consented to and affirmed psychic danger but not interference.

The last time the dream recurred he was so worried it might be true that he went into Father Quinlan's room to check. The old man lay breathing in a nylon sleeping bag that needed daylight to bounce the colour blue from one side and orange from the other, under a crucifix that was disgusting. Kuhlman thought that worship of a corpse was not OK. For this reason and to protect Father Quinlan from harm by himself he, Kuhlman, returned to his room, fastened his sandals which were made from lorry tyres, and picked up his pack.

The End

Father Quinlan became remiss not only in his bare feet but in his parish duties. He was retired to the Home where he died peacefully. Only the misinformed blamed his disappearance on the crazy lodger. The classification of sainthood or dementia awaits three miracles.

The next priest was hearty Father Ryan who installed central heating and kept his timetable on his computer.

In the market street, Kuhlman spotted a draggled blonde lurching round one of the stalls buying tartan leggings.

She said, 'Fuck off.'

'You fuck off.'

'I said "Fuck off" first.'

She had a bunch of twenties in her fist as she paid the stall woman for the leggings so he asked her, 'Is there anything about?' He had not given up his main and desperate search for the rape and transformation of his soul; he was resting.

Naked and Middle Aged

Evidently time moves at different speeds, fastest during the propitiating, morning rites. Even Dr Kuhlman defining time as the space between events and therefore not starting until the Big Bang, cannot explain how my morning ablutions wipe out so much time.

These rites are burdensome but compulsive. Bent under the burden, I can still sniff freedom. I have not given in.

Parenthetically, the label, or bar code, on Kuhlman's white coat, titles him Dr, but the coat fastens with poppers like the white coats of female catering workers. It could be the white overall of an immigrant packaging airline meals. The oil which burns in Kuhlman's eyes, which are the colour of dirty oil, is either holiness or fraud.

Body and mind are functions of each other; the space which contains the bone box should properly also contain the mind. The space, the one room, where I blunder from bed, is also the space where I think.

By extension, all life forms are functions of the planet. Air inflates the lungs; twenty years ago a wind from North Africa picked up desert sand and dropped it on London, where it was visible as red crystals on cars parked overnight.

How I Met the Devil

A slim, quick, hip young man lounged on the corner; also intrigued by the sand. He wore scruffy jeans, and a T-shirt with an arcane logo. His eyes were close set, which concentrated his holy-man focus. I was not his type of girl, but near enough his type. He offered me speed.

The sample, licked from my finger like sherbet, tasted bitter. A click in my head cancelled boredom; I was alert but null. My eyes were varnished, I did not blink when I looked at the sand which was no longer significant but only there, and sand. I kept up with Kuhlman, who ran in shabby trainers.

He fervently explained the serpent tattooed on his left arm.

'The snake believed that the knowledge of good and evil is higher than happiness. I'm a diabolist.'

He said he was crashing on friends' floors. However he gave me a card. His status surprised me:

DR KUHLMAN

How Will I Know if I Am Enlightened?

I cannot inhabit the mindset of a primitive form of the species: a creature with concepts for stone or tree, but not for arguing that non-existents may have properties but still be non-existent, such as the specifications for a devil. However the knowledge of good and evil proves fraudulent.

Alternatively the Fall could be upwards; knowledge delivered as revelation, significance like that of the muscular wind which hurled the red sand across continents. I look at nature, my fingers poke my mind, conscientiously checking, 'Am I in ecstasy? Is this an epiphany? Can I learn to fall upwards?'

I lie on my back in Kensington Gardens, in tall grass which tosses feathery tufts. The sky is oceanic, Prussian blue with wisps of white like the sea around an island. Altitudes are reversed.

The Devil with Thinner Hair and Thicker Waist

The hospital's original structure, and later wings, were surrounded by outbuildings housing various clinics, centres, units and departments. The weather was showery, the marble sky was melting into slush or vapour. A Portakabin had a card tacked to the door.

DR KUHLMAN

Below the name, some manic had scrawled:

Real cool, man

Twenty years on, he still flaunted a hip, fuck-you style but had gained gravitas and ex-wives. When I reminded him of knowledge versus happiness, he said, 'I was young, so my knowledge was about sex and drugs and café philosophy; did you ever go to The Hole or that piss hole under Charlotte Street? I was already a murderer. It happened like this. I was zigzagging along, in relatively harmless mode, when some idiot shouted at me across the road. It wasn't the first time I had received insults about my hair style or supposed sexual practices, but this guy called me a Social Security scrounger. I had trafficked in childish things, like drugs and stolen bikes and heisted jeans, but I had never signed on the dole. It was a point of vanity.'

My attraction to Kuhlman was ambivalent, in that I mistrusted his conviction of grievance which could invalidate the rest of his thinking.

He continued, 'I noticed how quickly I became vicious. I suppose the guy thought I was a skinny little runt, because he crossed the road to attack me. I killed him with a biro.'

'What happened?'

'Nothing happened. I was a fast runner and there was nothing to connect us. I killed because I was interested in my own viciousness and how far it would take me. I

47

wanted that knowledge. But when I looked outside the cafés, I realised that the world knowledge includes war and starvation and imprisonment and torture, and that unlike me, most victims had not chosen or agreed to their experiences. This questions the position of the diabolist. So here I am, in this hospital, doing good.'

The oil-burning eyes were sincere and untrustworthy. He wore sandals made from old tyres pitted by desert pilgrimage. Black hairs grew from his naked toes.

He said, 'I don't know how long I shall stay. The patients are either tedious or troublesome; you must meet Sonia. Basically I have a restless nature.'

On Deception, and the Killing and Eating of Gods

A principle of spite hides my socks, although they are a witty, fluorescent colour.

I scream at no God, 'You fucking shit, you arsehole in heaven, give me my socks back.'

The room is percussive with injustice.

On my next visit, Kuhlman again wore the tyre sandals, and a skinny, scuffed leather jacket over the womanish white coat.

Belief that $2 + 2 = 4$ carries a different intention from belief in democracy, and again from belief in God. One is about fact, the second about values, and the third about being or non-being. Phrases containing the word 'belief' should therefore be dismantled, and the units properly reassembled like the units in parsing, algebraic equations, and a drawer which contains all fluorescent lime socks and only fluorescent lime socks.

However, placing words does not alter my experience of the world. Rationally I believe, that if I put probability at 99%, the 1% allowing for an uncertainty factor such as a burglar who fancies sharp socks, that I am responsible.

48

Emotionally, I feel victimised by a malicious entity which mocks by hiding socks and other small objects, and by altering the speed of time.

When I described this paradox, or confusion, to Kuhlman, blasphemy and spittle flavoured with blue mouthwash flew from my lips. I was then distracted by a concept of a bumblebee which loomed, hovering, behind its triangular furry mask.

During my period of practising ape and australopithecine identities, David Attenborough's TV series about insects told me to become a creature whose external skeleton was a pod containing a bright green sap, but which performed complex tasks to conceal her eggs. Insect behaviour was proven deceptive. An insect's own grubs usurped by the grubs of a rival; a more complex ant sprayed a pheromone which made the victims attack each other instead of the invader.

'Do you keep bees here?'

'Virtual bees,' Kuhlman said. 'The therapist in the next cubicle treats phobias, behaviourally. He has his bee guy today. His arachnophobic guy is tomorrow.'

'I heard bees. Then I thought of other insects. It wasn't random. I don't know if there is free will.'

'Right, we'll allocate several sessions to discuss it seriously.'

'Free will may be possible for us, but not for insects. They are programmed to deceive. Deception is necessary for their survival and propagation. If deception exists in lower life forms, is nature false?'

'Nature is a fix between God and the devil,' Kuhlman insinuated. 'They are inseparable.'

The laws of physics were also infested.

Kuhlman was not shocked by dishonesty. He classed honesty as a commodity, sometimes affordable.

The word 'God' requires circumspection, as it need not include existence. There are also the gods of the second

49

part of my title, which refers to an antique and modern practice. When I was young, and on the scene, I shared ashtrays on café tables with elders who, being habitués of Soho and Fitzrovia, on seeing the poet plain, roaring from a bar stool among blaggers and belles dames sans mercenaries, reverently bought Dylan Thomas or Brendan Behan another drink. The sacrament of killing and eating gods is less direct through the newsprint priesthood which fattens footballers and musicians for communicants. As a fairly disgusting creature, and objective thinker, I have no rights to disapprove; however I'm personally uninterested in godliness by ingestion or proxy.

Disgust and Delight

Soon after dawn, strands of the colour orange unravel across the turquoise sky. My notes are titled ambiguously: ON TIME

Yesterday at the tube station, the indicator board showed: 'Circle Line 4 min'. I walked the platform before wheeling. The information was unchanged: 'Circle Line 4 min'.

The deception was blatant. Time mocks and confounds, treats unfairly, provokes. I suppressed my fury to a mutter.

'Fucking ludicrous.'

Nobody else protested; nobody else resented irrationality and injustice. Evidently MORNING HYPERSPEED has its antithesis, WAITING FOR A SPECIFIED TIME TO ELAPSE. However, some events occur in both contexts. I have identified (pun) CLEANING TEETH.

The savoury taste of the gums hints at the delights of the body's interior; the offals suffused with blood, the cellular bump and grind. I affirm my stinks and stews but compulsively neutralise each orifice.

50

Identifang

Animal species as diverse as flea, squid and elephant have an equipped head, system of ingesting, consuming and excreting, and enabling limbs. Neither species nor graphics, however grotesque, invent outside this plan. The intentional plan of vehicles copies the plan, whose degrees of intention are degrees of inevitability, of animals. If the plan is indeed inevitable, by tautology it also informs extra-terrestrial and extra-galactic species, and the species of parallel universes. If it is not, there is a possibility of species which are radically different, e.g. composed of more energy and less matter.

I realised, which is a different verb from knowing, that the teeth of reptiles and mammals were the teeth which picket my gums.

Cleaning teeth occurs in MORNING HYPER SPEED but I follow the dentist's instructions to brush for two minutes, i.e. I am WAITING FOR A SPECIFIED TIME TO ELAPSE. Time whines as it tries to engage both gears simultaneously. The whine must not be caused by my electric toothbrush; I am accustomed to move forward through the day by small explosions of will. I get up, I clean, I complete all errands and tasks, I am reliable.

Sonia, A Woman Scorned

Where there is a hospital waiting room, I sit on the addicts' side of the chair arrangement, or they choose me. I'm not their type, but recognised by them, therefore the young woman named Sonia aimed her grievances at me.

'That fucking cow won't give me my dustpan.'

She wore skinny jeans which boggled at the knees, and a shawl of black, netted yarn with soft hairy filaments like the legs of spiders. This outfit was attractive but most of her front teeth were missing.

The smug woman at the desk said, 'Doctor can't see you if you're late for your appointment.'

'I told you, my disabled bus pass got stolen. The fucking driver wouldn't let me on the fucking bus.'

Her dependency and abusive manner were fatal to her cause.

'They're all cows here. I want my dustpan.' She gripped my wrist, 'Excuse me darling.'

Her face, pale as a moth, was stained with amber bruises. She had sustained damage and neglect, she smelled of singeing.

I have few relationships and must analyse this which was forced upon me. I am cowardly, I can pass as normal and be complicit in banning creatures like Sonia, who risk and suffer for my instruction. Another consideration to address, is that both Kuhlman and Sonia noticed my outsider status and granted me almost equality. Possibly I am one of the saints, who will jazzily march in, unlike the self-righteous woman at the desk who wore a prissy blouse, parcelled in a bow under her chins, which reproved Sonia's chic, draggled furry cobweb. However I must be a saint by remove, without letting Sonia and her manipulative wants into my life.

Then something unexpected happened. Sonia let go of my wrist and fled to the reception desk. She buried her face in the woman's bloused breasts, and the woman cradled her in a manner that was partly competence and partly motherly.

I was confounded. I am misanthropic because I cannot love humanity when the weight of its numbers oppresses and depresses me. Humans are all over the streets, the parks. They lack rarity value. Now this woman, typical of the masses, nice, kind, reading behind her desk a tabloid newspaper specialising in swallowing small gods, was preferred, was canonised, before me.

I am a loner, unranked against the reception nurse almost certainly a wife and mother secure in the community. Loners notoriously mark out their territory in unpleasant habits, such as hoarding food waste or faeces in bin bags or paper parcels about the flat causing neighbours to complain of a sweetish stench. I cannot therefore wish for the support of the type; on the contrary my equilibrium rocks on the desire to be accepted by that humanity I dread and despise. The weight finally comes down to my refusal to countenance a pink blouse.

P2K4, The Chess Player's Car (Kuhlman)

I always knew the nature of Kuhlman's practice. Only psychiatric patients are sharp enough to graffiti a door; medical patients are slow on their bad legs. I had taken to dropping in at the Portakabin for the discussions I thought we both enjoyed.

Apparently he regards me as a patient, like Sonia. He cannot treat me because he has the inferior mind. His chess tactic is that an absurd move will throw his opponent. Certainly the first time he made one, I scoured the board for his plan. I even said, 'So! Vot is zis fiendish plot?'

His theory in this, and therefore possibly in other matters, is based on a misconception, an amazingly wrong idea. His wasted appearance, pilgrim sandals and close-set prophetic eyes disguise a mediocre mind. His integrity is in his experiments on himself.

In the Mouth of Hell and the Teeth of Time

There has been a fortnight's heatwave. A sirocco blew in through my open window. Pavement cafés were crowded. The fields of Kensington Gardens were brown as if covered with coir matting. I was exultant.

Eventually the temperature dropped but the power of inertia retained heat in earth, air and water. Even after three cold days, I turned a corner and encountered a pillar of heat in a form between energy and mass. Finally a North wind defeated the inertia and established its own rule of cold and inert cold. This cold coincided with the Sonia incident which denied my pretensions.

The bus stop nearest the hospital is on a thunderous dual carriageway. Vehicles continuously hurtle over a spur and onwards. Their roar continuously approaches, continuously breaks to the Doppler effect, and continuously recedes. A slip road feeds more traffic, from an industrial estate, onto the dual carriageway which is separated from the estate by a wire fence suspended between two concrete posts buffered by a hedge of privet pruned to its wooden springs.

No bus comes; they are possibly, but not provably, delayed because my Time Protester is in the pocket of my anorak; in semantics both a hooded waterproof jacket and that jacket's typically nerdy wearer. The Protester, in prototype form, is a chemist's bag containing toothbrush and paste and a bottle of stinging blue mouthwash. I am experimenting to hold time in slow gear. Either the experiment, or my sanity, will fail. They are eyeball to eyeball. My sanity doesn't blink, therefore I am not mad. I have neither proved nor disproved the instability of everything including time.

The metal-plated monsters charge down like mammoth and bison from an ice age. The industrial wind carries grits and rattles the plastic rags in the coils of the hedge. I am appalled by this place so desolate of nature. Energy leaks from my body and spirit flies out through the pineal eye. The debilitation is the reverse of the awe when I saw the red sand, soil of another climate.

I identify this bus stop as hell because I have been sheltered from the war, starvation, imprisonment and torture named by Kuhlman. Compared to the death of a child, mine is a lesser dissatisfaction in the permanently out-of-order complaints department of god. The note

54

sellotaped to the door of this department says: BACK IN 5 MINUTES; but on closer inspection it says: BACK IN 5 BILLION YEARS.

I struggle between despondency and the inept prodding of my brain to produce enthusiasm, Greek 'enthous' or 'inspiration by a god'.

Kuhlman understands and practises this principle. Its extreme practitioners die of excess. My nature is cautious but persistent: I need that something should be earned or learned here. A word is present but incorrect in my brain; I am an anorak wanting inspiration by an anoraknophobic God.

The woman who was part crocodile was formidable in her face armour of chained sunglasses and ear pendants. Her lower jaw grinned gently like the jawbone of a crocodile.

She lay partly submerged in the shallows of the river, where animals might cross, her coiffure erect against the watery reek of gases pulsing through the mud. She was unaware of causing the deaths of microscopic life forms – pods, spirals and larvae – which had been journeying by drifting, whiplashing, suction, and the ingestion and expulsion of water, until impeded by her bulk to perish in the folds of her clothing.

In her heyday she had bitten into politics and economics. Now 70, she wrote snappish letters, using Greek e's, complaining of the tax on her dividends and of mosquitoes.

One day Dr Kuhlman came to the river bank. His late mother had been her friend and colleague but she had never trusted the son.

Kuhlman was 50 but looked younger due to his disgraceful lifestyle and active mind. He wore a soiled medical coat over, also soiled, T-shirt and jeans. He seemed exhausted but further wasted himself by sniffing, blinking and scratching, which exhibited the schizophrenia of fatigue. He read and handed back one of the protesting letters saying, 'Of course they draw blood. They're mosquitoes, it's their job to draw blood. Their world centres on mosquitoes as yours centres on old ladies. Why complain?'

He continued persuasively, 'Nobody crosses the river here any more. They're all splashing upstream. You should move into the Sunset Home where I have worked for at least three weeks. I can fix you a discount.' When he mentioned money, points of holy fire lit in Kuhlman's eyes, which were the colour of dirty oil. 'The cake trolley comes round at teatime.'

'Does it have banana cheesecake?'
'Yes,' he lied.

She sat in an orthopaedic chair facing the TV whose channel was fixed by management override. She quite enjoyed the children's programmes, but missed the political discussions. At all times she clutched her shares portfolio on which she kept the shrewd eye of a crocodile or an urban peasant. Her claw on the folder was scaly with nails painted in Schiaparelli's shocking pink. Her lower jaw ground on its hinges when she thought of biting Dr Kuhlman.

On his next round, however, Kuhlman pulled a hard chair up to hers. Temple oil burned fervently in his eyes and a tattooed snake climbed his left arm.

He said, 'There have been complaints. Other patients bitten; the bathroom flooded. You must leave.'

'You have taken your percentage of my deposit.'

'I'm a criminal. I've spent it.'

'Scoundrel! Vile seducer!'

'Surely, Madam, even at my most extreme I didn't?'

'Certainly not. That's not what I meant. I went through my wardrobe and gave two blouses, good quality, to that fool who pushes the cake trolley. There is no banana cheesecake, so I am supposed to tell her the blouses were a sale not a present?'

'As you please. I took your money through boredom, or depravity. It was on a whim to make an old dear from an old crocodile bag.' He giggled at his joke. 'I didn't take much. Anyway money is virtual. Let me make amends by giving you, at no cost, some advice. You and my mother worked in an office for years. Now you are free to achieve true sanctity as I am a saint of experience. I love experience, I'd snort it, smoke it, if I was a woman I'd swallow its come. Excuse me. I think you will never be a saint of experience but you could be a saint of economics. Don't wallow in the river making trivial complaints. Write your book on economics. I speak with the utmost sincerity.'

'I always knew you were a crook. Where is your mother's garnet bracelet she promised me?'

Many women in Kuhlman's life had been exciting, unscrupulous and needy. He had forgotten which one he had given, or allowed to steal, the garnet bracelet.

When young, Kuhlman had been thrilled by his own malice, by its swift arrival and limitless extremes. It was rumoured he had killed a man using only a ballpoint pen. Later he had experimented with saintly actions, which were equally interesting. Horns and halo were interchangeably wild.

His divided soul of a swindler considered dishonesty as training parallel to and meeting only at infinity his vow of poverty. Like a mendicant pilgrim he moved on. His few possessions, already half packed, included books, rubber sandals made of old tyres, and a tin box of little value whose lid was enamelled with the same serpent.

He promised, valuably or without value, to contact an educational publisher he knew and suggest that a work on political economy be commissioned from his mother's old friend who had research, mostly on Russia and Eastern Europe, stored on her computer. That she was at present greedy and selfish made her rescue agreeably perverse. His embrace of her would further exhaust or sensationalise him.

Unfortunately the woman did not comprehend his form of attribution, and ignored his advice on the childish and prejudiced grounds that its author was a follower of the devil.

She returned to the river and threw herself in with a flop that displaced a spout of water which contained disc-shaped transparencies, showing digestive and vascular threads, which fell on the mud flats pock-marked by implosions, where they died.

By the same momentum, winged insects, including a beetle, which had been stuck, struggling, to the skin of the water, were released.

WHERE IS MY MASK OF AN HONEST MAN?

Death of a Pigeon

— I propose to consider the question, what is morality?

Mostyn Road, NW10, was a side street of two-storey brick houses, built 1908, some of which had been divided into flats. A ground-level property was vacant between lettings. The front room was bare-floored and unfurnished but contained a polar sleeping bag, a whisky bottle, four modern first editions strapped within a webbing belt and an oil painting on a 12" x 18" board. These objects belonged to the landlord, Harry Brightling, who was camping on site.

Outside, on the grassy patch before a brick wall at knee height, were one dustbin, two sacks of builders' cement, one pavement-hued pigeon and one fox whose breath smelt of starvation and whose high trot weighed scarcely more than its bones; which units could by ruthless adventure be redistributed so that the future economy of the yard would be one dustbin, two cement sacks, one fleet movement and a mash of bloody spines.

— The survival of the fox depends on the death of the pigeon. This will come within my consideration.

Brightling was 38 but looked younger because he was slim and had kept his hair, which was straight, silky and dark brown. His face was oval, not handsome but pleasing: a neutral ground like the face of an actor who wipes off with vanishing cream the mask of Macbeth or Iago to reveal a face that is pale, cleansed, glittering and wearied. He wore an old Turnbull and Asser shirt and democratic jeans.

He was at present rehearsing the part of landlord, owning two properties of which 19 Mostyn Road was the lesser. His other amateur and provisional role was antiques dealer.

Two years ago, his friend Morgan, in selling on a painting to another dealer, had greatly exaggerated the price he himself had paid for it. Morgan, appropriately, was a piratical rogue, 6'4" in height. His grizzled hair was ringleted like a Caroline wig which in high wind became a foppish pompadour. The other dealer, discovering the deception, had decided to sue. Morgan's lawyer's defence would be to freely admit her client's misrepresentation but point out that such inflation was standard practice within the trade. All dealers, including the claimant, would expect and allow for it. This courtroom ambush required corroborating testimony from two other, reasonably presentable, dealers. Through delight in escapade, and to distract from a red-haired croupier whom he had overestimated, Brightling had been one of them. Afterwards the team had celebrated with oysters.

Plainly his part had required duelling with a dishonourable sword; however, in an epiphany on the way to a taxi rank, he had decided that if his impersonation did not coincide with the good, the good must be repositioned.

Exhilarating dawn raids on markets or car boot sales contained a negative, or traitor. The shape of the traitor was that the trafficker in antiques, i.e. Brightling, competitively hunts the unique through sites swept by wind, rain and mercenaries in cash-wadded anoraks. He, Brightling, therefore experiences the mortification of losing to a rival, or its gloating reverse, which equally exhaust the spirit. His adopted profession was treacherously enervating.

He said to the bottle, — The spirit is exhausted.

The 19th century oil painting, which he had bought at 4.30 this morning from a van unloading, was of a monkey in a scarlet military jacket who was gripping a cat, used literally as a cat's paw to pick roasting chestnuts from a griddle. The picture's furniture, such as a stool, an apple and a jug, was painted realistically. The animals were grotesques. The monkey, with whose cause Brightling identified, grinned with experimental glee.

Books and pictures had been brought to Mostyn Road in what he described to himself as a getaway car, under a blanket. Their purchaser was fit, sharp and laid waste.

— Fuck all distinctions. The good is whatever buys whisky and decent shirts.

Leaving the house, he encountered a short, stout, ruddy, retarded man. Tom Shadwell worked on Portobello Market, where he waddled hugging boxes of fruit and vegetables and clambered into vans. He was surprisingly strong and agile. He wore a filthy anorak. Brightling cast him as a descendant of those tumblers and clowns whose performances were written into 16th-century drama: rude blasphemous players whose antics broke up the business of Faust and Mephistopheles.

'Ar-oh.'

'No, Tom. *Arsehole*. You must learn to enunciate. You can't come in, I'm leaving.'

'Ar-oh,' said Tom cheerfully. He showed his backside while bending to scoop the late pigeon into the *Metro*.

Brightling's appointment was at his more interesting investment. He had gambled on the top floor, which was a one room with bathroom, of a Victorian house in Notting Hill. It was devalued by a protected tenant.

Portrait of an Author

Joan Byker, 78, treated the composition of prose like one of the coprophiliac arts that used clay or tubes of pigment. Her green wirebound books were synaesthetic, being defaced or decorated with crossings-out and words in loops or margins wired into the text. The final logic was anything left standing. Her style was analytical but anal; of the mud-pie school of literature. She had had a novel published in the days of her youth when all a writer needed was cigarettes and seriousness, and publishers sat behind the desk behind the door that had their name on it. If one put in the talent and the work, the house was accessible.

Each morning when woken by birdsong she girded herself with the rallying cry 'Shit out; teeth in', showing a preoccupation with hygiene; also to start the day before the possibility of dismay set in.

In appearance she was jolly, weather-reddened, academic, raw-boned. On the occasions of a visit by the new landlord she wore a tweed skirt, baggy black jumper, and school socks and sandals. She received him with her legs braced apart, like a fielder.

'Ms Byker? Harry Brightling. Angel have you any coffee? I've been up all night and on to a market in Kent. I bought some books. I see you're a reader.'

In the sexually aroused, businesslike manner of burglars and dealers, he assessed the furniture and other contents. The room seemed to belong to a clever but underdeveloped student: physical or emotional naivety looked out of her eyes. The many books included hikers' guides of the *Walks around Surrey* sort and also leaflets for a wetland centre or Norman church. By their condition, the *Oxford Etymological Dictionary, the Penguin Dictionary of Physics and the Keble Martin Concise British Flora* seemed much consulted. Green wirebound exercise books were piled on a chair. A cooker, a sink and a fridge shaking with ague were in neglected collage. There was also a plastic bucket.

On an amateur nature table, she had collected rocks like lower jaws with quartz teeth. Other rocks contained the fossilised imprints of molluscs and ferns. Twigs of fossilised wood were in the process of spontaneously combusting into ash and pyritic phosphate fumes more acrid than woodsmoke.

She said, 'Don't touch that or you'll smell of it all day. Millions of years old incendiary stink. If I'd known that

64

the wood was unstable I'd have left it on the beach where I found it.'

Brightling treated wherever he was as a club of which he was a member. He took it as his right to hold a magnifying glass to a painting. His hands were not clean; compromised but graceful.

Joan was gratified by his interest in her belongings. She also liked his dissolute, sour-apple taint of whisky and the dark oily base of bergamot from which the higher notes had worn off; and the narrow black shoes whose high tight lacing puckered the supple leather. Footwear so gentlemanly could not fit a cloven hoof.

She heated water in a saucepan.

He said, 'Sorry to arrive so actually shattered. I've a habit of gambling clubs or walking at night.' The coffee which she gave him dissolved the gritty crystals of fatigue which itched and flashed behind his eyeballs. 'I cut down on sleep.'

She enthused, 'Like Johnson and Savage. Of course they could walk and talk across 18th-century London in two hours. Now the city roars with the voice of dinosaurs, megalosaurian buildings rear up, herds of hypsilophodonts flee through the streets; archaeopteryx soars overhead. Did you say you were a gambler?'

'Yes. But I gave up the club. The story is discreditable; I should not tell you.'

'Oh, do.'

'Very well.' He prepared to entertain. In extremis he could perform a soft shoe shuffle. He leaned forward. 'I was besotted by a red-haired croupier. One night I turned up at her place with a bottle. Actually it was half a bottle.'

'Half a bottle?'

'I was better looking then and could get away with it. In the morning it turned out we were not alone. She had a child, a two-year-old princess in a pink nightie.'

Joan Byker angled Talmudic reasoning at this story. 'Who looked after the child when the mother was at the club?'

'The grandmother would stay the night. Anyway, during cornflakes, the phone rang. It was another mother asking about a playgroup. Joan, in that moment I saw that her plans for me were tame man in her single mothers' group. I never went back, to the club or to the flat.'

'You missed the club?'

'Of course. But antiques dealing is a gamble. I should have brought the books I mentioned to show you. One of them is signed by the author.'

'Which makes it more valuable according to the magic belief that virtue exists and is transferable from person to object.'

'We think alike. The antiques trade turns on transferable virtue; from person to object as you said, and also of course from historical decades and centuries to the present. Virtue separates an 18th-century table or an art deco pot from their reproductions or fakes. It's romantic theory expressed in terms of money, don't you think?' He tempted, 'Now tell me something about yourself.'

'Well, when I was at school I usually got the answers right because the questions were logical. Parsing a sentence or solving an equation are exercises in logic: one concentrates and works them out. Also the noun "student" has no gender. I was OK as a subject, but it turned out I was no good as an object.'

'No good at what, Joan? I may call you Joan?'

'Men; and fucking. Yes, you may. I was useless at all that. A complete dud. Now I'm old I'm free to do my own thing again.' She gazed inspirationally upwards as if her palm balanced a leather netball and the girls in shorts shouted, 'Shoot, shoot', and finally, 'Goal!' She herself shouted, 'Freedom!'

In metaphor or legend she had regained the power of virginity.

He said, 'I must introduce my girlfriend to you. She'd be more helpful.'

'Not the same one?'

'Absolutely not.'

'This one is childless?'

'Definitely. She has a career. What's that bucket for?'

'Bucket? Oh, the bucket. The ceiling leaks.'

He said, 'I'll have a look. How do I get onto the roof?'

There was a gulley, a shallow metal trough carpeted with tarred canvas. Leaves and other matter had degraded into a dam of sludge, causing brackish liquid to seep through. He called down for bin bag and broom. Waiting, he noticed that fatigue produced numbness, as if he had been nursed or persuaded into a padded jacket. He willed himself awake by concentrating on the sky which shone as far as he could see from Shepherds Bush to Paddington. Joan's mention of the poets brought to his mind the succeeding generations of provincials arrived in the city. The exceptional ones had instantly recognised the café, jazz club, bar or hole in the wall that was the scene, the hangout, the place to be which took them seriously. Somewhere below the streets were splintered by the sound of a pick on masonry. His tenant would confuse romantic with sentimental at her peril. Harry Brightling was, definably, only romantic.

When he had gone, Joan felt nourished by the flattery implicit in the intimacy which had been established between them. They had exchanged unusual confidences. He had a pleasing manner of referral: 'Do you think?' or 'Don't you think?' Conversely she reserved the right to suspect his charm; to think him an operator.

She observed the bees which were hunched like bison on the clover and knapweed in the windowbox. The windowbox contained wild flowers and tall grass, like a strip of the idyllic hay meadow of a 1930s, precisely positioned middle-class childhood. She was ecstatic at the colour violet which streamed, narrow as a laser beam, from meadow clary; and much interested in the jade escutcheon and transparent feelers of an insect that climbed a grass stem.

She brushed down her arm in the action of the man whose saintly sullied hand had brushed roof dirt from his sleeve. She had flinched when he had mentioned a girlfriend but she concluded that of course he had a woman. Sexually and emotionally she had regressed to the adolescence of a crush on a film star. She had a crush on, or pash for, Harry Brightling.

On leaving Joan in Vernon Crescent, Brightling strolled the short distance down Portobello Road to an arcade. His mouth contained a taste that was like the air on a tube platform: stale, invigorating, insomniac.

Behind a scarlet and gold façade, the arcade opened, trumpeted out, into kiosks and stalls. An impeccably suited African dealt in silver-plated teapots. Two women offered used frocks and handbags under a handwritten sign VINTAGE. A Turkish middle-aged man sold T-shirts with slogans such as I SOLD MY SOUL FOR ROCK AND ROLL. The jewellery kiosk and the counter of London photographs were closed.

He entered rhetorically demanding, 'Where's my costume, where's my music, where did I leave my mask of an honest man?'

Buying delivered an adrenalin rush. Selling, unless to an interesting customer, bored him. For this reason his collection, which mixed books with mocking or grotesque objects including a witch doctor's shabby wand, and a group of nomili, stunted humanoids in stone from Sierra Leone, was looked after by a Polish woman whose two well-behaved children could do their homework at the back of the arcade. The employment of Krystina was a charitable action or cynical gambit. Brightling was ambiguous; Krystina was loyal and grateful.

The accepted greeting among traders was a variant on, 'Any good?' such as, 'How you done? Any good?' The question was vulgar but the reply required delicacy. There was finessing; a swimming motion of the hand. It was tactful to line up with the others; to take similar totals; to incur neither envy nor pity. Only Brightling unblinkingly boasted. His effrontery either was or was not deception.

'Krystina have we any money? Excellent; I knew that German would come back for the fairground Punch.'

The seller of T-shirts said, 'Health and Safety wants to close this arcade.'

'Selfish bastards with no thought for the unhealthy and unsafe.' Brightling enjoyed the camaraderie; the feeling that others, to whom he was almost entirely indifferent, were good sorts.

A 1960s, low-slung Jaguar E-type slouched along the kerb. The back seat was covered by a blanket used to wrap pictures. The woman driver, mid-thirties, appeared pleasant, natural, fair-minded and brave. Cleanliness from forehead to fingernails was due to either soap and water or costly products. Her short springy hair was the colour of electric wheat. She wore a silk camisole, and jeans splashed with decorators' emulsion.

Maud Percival moved law books from the passenger seat for Brightling to get into the car. When it had gone its lion cough hung in the air.

On a Goat's Beard

Joan Byker's next contact with her unusual new landlord was when he phoned her. Loud music was in the background. Some of the words were –'that's my baby dressed in red'. He had been so interested in their conversation, he said, that he had forgotten to tell her the account number into which she was to pay the rent and, more importantly, to discuss the leaking gulley. He was not, he apologised, a businessman. He felt, didn't she, that they were friends. He would come at three.

When he had rung off, she thought –that's my baby dressed in red. However she looked at the plants in the window box and wrote in her exercise book:

On A Goat's Beard

Goat's beard exists, goes through its cycles, on its own terms. It passes itself off as a clump of grass until the blade thickens. The thickness travels up the stem then opens until midday as a golden crown encircled by green spikes. Next day, the same event. Then nothing for a fortnight. Then it reopens as a boldly spoked and feathered dandelion clock whipping in the wind like the demented hair of Einstein. Its leaves, sparse whiskery pennants, could indeed be the horns, beards and prancing hooves of goats. It is a biennial.

She was on principle severe on mixed metaphor but had wished to praise the plant. No trouble was too much for her to humour its idiosyncrasies. She next repositioned and replanted the clump which should perform next year. She inhaled from her hands the pungent reek of earth.

She had been eighteen when she had devised black nail varnish. Until it chipped she had been black-nailed in Soho cafés and clubs. The man she wanted to impress, coincidentally also named Harry, had possessed un-shallow charm in the manner of Harry Brightling. At base he could not be bothered with a healthy-faced girl with one foot in Soho and the other in the Wimbledon Girl Guides. Her writing at the time had been for him; from the girl genius hybrid in cotton frocks and black nails.

It would be inappropriate to present *On a Goat's Beard* to Harry. She did not want a man to breach her body or her porridge-eating, reading and lavatorial routines. However she was reminded of her youth when her hands had been Soho not gardening. Since knowing Harry the dismay had retreated.

He arrived sporting a jacket with a pinched-in cut, which was properly the jacket of a business suit, over jeans and a T-shirt that was flakily stamped I Sold My Soul for Rock and Roll. One high-arched, high-laced, subtle gentlemanly shoe nudged the door ajar while he called, 'Is the coffee on?' Once inside, he turned out of his pockets seven: default was inevitable: tarnished turned handles which, he explained, he had appropriated from an auction viewing against his intentions to bid for their chest of drawers.

'Are they original? What do you think, Joan?'

As she wore an ancient Irish tweed skirt with petersham waistband and hooks and eyes hand sewn with unmatching cotton thread into the placket, Joan Byker demonstrably had an instinct for quality and style. She acknowledged his spivvy jacket. He might have bought it from a second-hand stall. One needed an eye for such things. She had not yet decided whether the shoes were English or Italian.

If he were playing a farce he would apologise for his delay in evicting her. He would plead exhaustion due to too much sex and too much work. However the curtain must rise.

'Angel, I've spoken to the other tenants and it seems the roof is sound. Only the gulley needs resurfacing. Tell me, should we do something about the ceiling? Don't you find the damp stain rather depressing?'

'Here's your coffee. Oops, sorry to barge. I was thinking about metaphor. Of course in prose composition there are rules but you can break them.'

'In the arts, yes I agree, but not in property maintenance.' Enacting the fall of the ceiling he used his hands like a working actor: a man hired by the hour to play a man. 'I know a reliable builder who could bring it down and replaster.'

71

'Lot of dust.'

'We'd have to cover the furniture. I would especially take down and wrap that boat picture.'

'Boats on the Volga. From the Stalinist era when artists worked for the state.'

'It should have its certificate of release on the back.'

'Like a prisoner. Yes, it has.'

'But basically we'd have to temporarily move you and most of the furniture out.'

'Where to?'

'Fortuitously I own another flat quite near. It's just been done up, it's empty.'

'I should stay here because one of my wildflowers has seeded in the area below. White Campion. If I don't watch the tenant will pull it up. People think they're weeds. Murderers! The seed pods of Campion are beautiful. Striped longitudinally, somewhat fuzzy. Looking at one is jolly ecstatic. I don't generally mention it, but when I look at plants it's like being on acid. You're taking the piss.'

'Absolutely not but I'm totally urban. Let me be upfront with you. The address of the other flat is not so smart. But it has a garden which backs onto the garden of the next street. There are squirrels and foxes. It would be perfect for you. In fact, I don't want anyone else to have it.'

'Foxes?'

'A dog fox, quite blatant, in daytime.'

'I'd like a garden.'

'Of course you would. You could stay there while this place is repaired. Or permanently exchange. Joan, you must attend carefully. Are you attending? I'm speaking as landlord and friend. You pay registered rent here. I'll give you the garden flat at the same rent.'

Joan had no talent for immediate experience. It existed only when retold to herself. Consequently she wished him gone in order that she could write in her exercise book his qualities using adjectival nouns, e.g. courtesy, mockery, incitement and complicity. She had noticed from the start the dissonance whereby he was at once frank and duplicitous. There was something Shakespearian about his gestures as if he were handling the crown of Richard III or the skull of Yorick. Her breasts like soft torpedoes swung uselessly inside the black jumper.

He said, 'My girlfriend is a lawyer and can draw up a contract guaranteeing that I will never raise the rent on the garden flat. I could of course get double from anyone else.'

'Aren't you jealous of all those big bank robbers?'

'She practises civil law, not criminal. In fact I met her when she was representing a friend: a complete swindler whose idea of a suave approach to a woman is "You've got a lovely mouth for sucking cock".'

Joan said, 'Sorry, I never swallow on a first date.'

Harry Brightling had not lied but his presentation had contained a falsity as egregious as Tom Shadwell in jester costume stained under the armpits.

— I'm wasted playing all these parts. Programme, madam? Fucking chocolates?

The Feet of Insects

Joan Byker, with some but not all of her effects, including wirebound exercise books of slaughtered words, was delivered to Mostyn Road by furniture van.

The driver, Morgan, was a sickle moon of a man; a concavity between grizzled ringlets; a time-zapped lengthy Stuart cowboy in leather gilet and flared jeans.

She asked, 'Have you known Harry long?'

A Texan-heeled boot kicked the accelerator.

The driver's mate, Tom Shadwell, reacted enthusiastically to Harry's name. He had a speech impediment and uttered the short 'a' and the 'ee' with

73

approval while rolling like a ruddy apple or muddy turnip against the side of the van.

Soon she was installed and living in her temporary home.

She wanted little except books and plants although she was occasionally impassioned by good quality socks or jumpers. Her platonic idea of a kitchen was undeveloped past the student cooker in a corner. She was amazed that other people upgraded their kitchens: why give oneself such trouble twice? In Mostyn Road's new kitchen she used one burner and washed up in the sink. The windows swung an arc so she must put the Vernon windowboxes in the back garden. The medieval jousting pennants and prancing skeletal goatery of tragopogon pratensis were desiccated but aloft.

As to the back garden, grass had recently been unrolled over a thin friable compound of earth and rubble. Castor oil and other evergreen shrubs gloomed the narrow beds along the fences. There was a Regency pedestal urn in white plastic whose electromagnetic field attracted particles of cosmic dust.

Joan had not yet decided whether to stay permanently and therefore did not work in the garden although exercise, along with regular bowel movements, held off the dismay or dread which she daily managed her life to avoid. Dismay was specific to areas which mixed blandness with horror, such as suburban streets or ranks of mean housing. It was the dismay of sameness. At 19 Mostyn Road sameness inhabited the objects around her; thus the lawn of reflective grass blades shone with ordinariness and sunlight travelled 92 million miles to sparkle in each piece of grit of the gravelled wall of the neighbours' kitchen extension.

Mostyn Road, the side street off a bus route, the parade of boxy windows, dismayed with its supra-ordinariness that left her spirits run out like water from a bath. She walked down to the main road and noticed, beneath the screen of the bus stop which was opposite but slightly downhill, a pair of feet in Nike trainers, and a set of feet like the four of clubs, which on reaching the bus stop shelter she discovered belonged to a youth and his black Staffordshire terrier and caused her to consider varieties of foot such as paw, hoof and claw.

Later that day she phoned Harry. 'I've been to the Natural History Museum to look at the feet of insects. Prongs, hooks, barbs and suction pads. It's fascinating.'

'Joan.'

'Claws. They're arthropods, like lobsters.'

'Joan.'

'Yes?'

'Why did you look at insects?'

'I was struck by the specifications in the design of feet. What is consistent and what is different. Insects are particularly interesting. And to avoid the dismay.'

'Dismay?'

'It's like being stuck in the present moment and thinking, this is all there is. This is the intersection of infinity with Mostyn Road.'

'Oh, that dismay. A large whisky helps.'

'Writers must keep a clear mind.'

'Dealers have only to be less totalled than the others.'

'Harry.'

'I'll take you out for a drink quite soon. How's the garden?'

'The castor oil plant started the dismay. Shrubs depress me. Of course it has been argued that all actions are escapes from boredom.'

'So does that remove the heroism from a hero or the virtue from good or bad deeds? You are saying, and I agree, that boredom is stale energy. We are very alike, Joan. And if you stay in the garden flat I'll dig up the shrubs for you. You shan't be bored or depressed.'

She said, 'What about my ceiling?' but he had switched off.

Little did she know that Brightling was speaking from her own flat and that nothing had been done about its ceiling. He lay on its floor in a slain position, resting his head on Maud Percival's lap, a bar of sunlight across his body in the shape of an axe, declaiming the sum of money expected from the property's sale. He was working, for he held in one hand a penknife, in the other a small framed drawing.

Encamped with Maud, temporarily, he was entertained on workday mornings when, her warm body concealed by crisp white blouse, black skirt and black zigzag-cut Vivienne Westwood coat, she ran downstairs holding her shoes and briefcase until she reached the street and threw them into the taxi, with regular driver, that waited for her. The taxi would pause at the corner for her to buy cappuccino. Brightling also approved that Maud took on his friends without trying to hold his interest by flirting with them. She was on the level; spiritually clean. Her cooking had, also temporarily, rescued him from the fiery takeaways that next day danced a tango in his arse. He did not tell her that his sequestering of this flat was illegal because Maud was the daughter of a class that could afford honesty: a recipient of music lessons, tennis lessons and honesty. Although she met dishonesty in her profession, by privileged dissonance she held on to hauteur. He, Brightling, did not.

He considered the need to keep Joan Byker away until her removal was an accomplished fact. He could either, as now, do nothing about the ceiling or bring it down to make the place uninhabitable. Meanwhile he had not solved the anomaly of his trade. He inspected the drawing, of a crow in pen and ink on vellum, which he had dislodged from its frame.

He said, 'Do you like it? It's very fine isn't it?'

The trade pursuit of such fineness damaged the pursuer. He had witnessed two dealers squabbling over a plate. Because his almost daily plot was the hunt and its catharsis, he sold things on while laughing like a gargoyle. While they were in his possession however he wanted to enjoy them. His instinct to fly high was therefore to live in, not to sell, this flat which was more congenial than the furniture storage lock-up with foam mattress at the back which Morgan, whenever borrowing it, called 'Harry's shag pad'.

To Act is to Choose

Next day Joan was on the top deck of a bus held up by traffic lights. She saw two men carrying a chest of drawers into an antiques shop. One was Morgan, the emaciated driver who had delivered her to Mostyn Road. The other, more graceful, his sleeves pushed back, was Harry.

The shop door was held open by a blonde who wore, outrageously and naturally, gaberdine breeches and a cashmere jumper. Morgan, who had grudged speaking to Joan, seemed more at ease with the blonde whose qualities of remove and being one of the gang were high-ranking cool. Joan also recognised their van, parked a few yards uphill. She craned as the bus window became blurred by sudden rain.

From this moment she became preoccupied by their three-ness. She regretted that she had not made an effort to talk to Morgan. She could have been witty. She speculated about Harry's woman who wore unusual clothes without apology. The breeches were cuffed and buttoned at the knee.

She now had the responsibility of emotionally stalking not only Harry but his friends.

By prerogative Brightling had himself chauffeured, in Maud's old Jag or Morgan's van.

He was cushioned by hangover. Last night it had seemed a good idea to buy Curry Goat with Red One Sauce from a shack that had PHIL U painted on its window; and to do so accompanied by Morgan who was ignorant that the one house rule of an otherwise tolerant establishment was that no customer, under any circumstances, was to be given a free bag. Phil and Morgan had debated his point in towering crescendos of unreason. Dominos had shuddered on the tables. Finally Morgan had pirouetted in the doorway in the arabesque of a drunk trying to remember whether he was fighting or leaving. He had held a torn bag.

Brightling had said, 'At least we'll be welcome next time we come.'

Now flagella-tailed raindrops swam horizontally across the windscreen, beyond the papers of clearance and delivery addresses and a kitsch wooden plaque showing a poker-burnt outline of Cornwall. Morgan was Cornish; the accent shared his speech with street-market mouth and fake American. He observed, 'Like sperm, man, like sperm.'

The next time she phoned Harry, Joan said, 'Joke. The barman said, "Sorry, we don't serve neutrinos here". A neutrino went into the bar.'

'Oh, Joan, right. How splendid to hear from you. There's been some delay, not serious, on the ceiling at Vernon. Good if you stay where you are. Garden all right?'

'Heigh-ho.'

This was the second phone call in which, by uncertainty or random disequilibrium, she had not spoken her decision to stay. To act is to choose. The action of speaking would determine the choice. She had received the second half of her yearly pension and had bought two books, by authors who delivered pleasure as soon as she opened their new novels, read the introductory sentences and inhaled the woody smell of the paper. The spending also possible, on the garden, would include an excursion to British Wild Flower Plants in Norfolk. On her last visit there had been an interesting discussion with a lepidopterist who was buying the rare food plants of his caterpillars. To look up the train times would in effect be an act of choosing to stay. To act as if she were to stay would be to stay.

Meanwhile there was the dismay whereby the neighbours' gravelled wall was permanent and unstable, like a DVD forever on pause.

She had noticed that Morgan's van sometimes passed the house. He must live, or have parking space, nearby. His times were morning and accordingly she positioned herself, a safe hour in advance, behind the boxy window of the front room. Sometimes the position she held caused an ache in her right leg. She recognised his van by the wooden plaque of the county of Cornwall that leant, amongst papers, against the windscreen. On one occasion, Harry had been in the passenger seat. She had rewarded herself with a cup of coffee. Unfortunately she did not know where to station herself to sight the woman.

During one vigil, she noticed a For Sale board on a house opposite. Suddenly she understood the circumstances which could make her homeless. Her mind blanked with the white noise of shock.

What Happened on the Roof

She put on her army jacket. She left the house and walked down the street. She smiled pleasantly at passers-by. She waited at the bus stop where she had noticed the feet of owner and dog. She boarded the bus. She was courteous in the matter of seats and other passengers' shopping. As the bus descended the hill her face showed the imperturbable politeness, the serene affability of one setting off to commit suicide or murder although her own irrevocable act was lesser. It was to go home.

Her key did not fit. Evidently the front door lock had been changed. She rang all bells and waited. Then she stepped next door and rang the bell of the top floor flat which mirrored her own. She explained to its tenant that she had been locked out and requested the use of his trapdoor through which she could access the roof and her own trapdoor. She ignored the buzzing noise which must be his protests and asked that he held the ladder steady.

On the roof, she advanced, crouching, between parapet and tiles. She wrote an essay in her mind.

— Those who live past seventy pay their due in chronic discomfort. From the Greek, chronos, time. As in chronicle, chronometer, synchronise, etc. I have adapted to tolerate pain but resent the tedium of the pain caused by for e.g. climbing stairs or carrying shopping. For every sack of washing brought home I must as it were climb a steep hill. Hurrying is a schizoid activity: the body is detained in place X while desire has raced to place Y. The old are imprisoned longer than the others in this condition of the body struggling uphill against the wind while the spirit has reached home and at last, please God, a piss. The worst is going upstairs while carrying shopping and wanting to piss. Fuck sake I can't want to piss here on the roof in my new fleecy leggings. Ending the essay, she recited, 'Two plus zero equals two; two minus zero equals two; two multiplied by zero equals zero; two divided by zero equals infinity.'

Brightling heard the clatter on the tiles before he saw Joan Byker slide down the ladder. A fold of material suggested that the tweed skirt held up knickers or other undergarments.

He was annoyed but said, 'Have you been admiring the view from the roof?'

No work had been done on the ceiling. Her remaining property had been shoved aside for the triumphant bivouac of Harry Brightling. The computer, briefcase and two unopened packs of Wolford tights evidently belonged to his woman, who was wearing a teal tube of cashmere over the breeches and holding a book.

Joan put on her glasses to read the title. 'Oh, do you like him?'

'Harry bought it in a lot of modern firsts. I'm Maud. Yes, do you?'

'I'm Joan. Yes, especially this one. Influences of Dostoevsky and Canetti. I would suppose first novels are the most influenced.'

'I must think about that.'

Brightling said, 'What the actual fuck?'

Joan said, 'Get out of my place. I know what your game is.'

'Do I have a game?'

'Any rent contract on Mostyn would be between you and me. You could sell the flat and I'd have no contact with the new owner.'

Maud said, 'Legally she's right. Controlled rent applies only to this property.'

Brightling said, 'What suspicious minds you both have.'

Joan said, 'You changed the front door lock.'

'Not at all. One of the tenants got her handbag stolen. The lock was changed for security. All tenants have new keys. You can have yours whenever you want.'

'You didn't answer the bell.'

'Angel, I was asleep. My hours are eccentric.'

Maud said, 'I arrived while you were on the roof. I haven't unpacked the shopping yet.'

Two cardboard boxes contained bottles of wine, balsamic vinegar and olive oil. There were also cheeses, eggs, avocados, salads, oranges and soured cream. A brown paper wrap spilled organically grown vegetables: dark green leaves with ivory veins and a smear of reddish mud; swedes stained purple, yellow and green.

Maud said, 'You must have dinner with us. I need to work for an hour, then we can eat.'

Joan said, 'I'm going to the lavatory.'

Maud said, 'What have you done?'

Brightling said, 'Nothing. I'm innocent. Well, more or less. Total shite, I thought she liked me.'

In her own bathroom, having emptied her bladder with a voluptuous sigh, Joan examined Maud's bottles of essential oils and extract of seaweed. She did not touch a disc of brown soap with dried foam on it.

Returned, she saw the radiantly beautiful vegetables had equality with other foreground objects which happened to be the blurred fabric and freckled buttons of Maud's breeches. Maud was now barefoot. Unexpectedly her feet were middle aged:; long and rather puffy. Joan knew that this moment of affirmation of all within sight was due to the presence of Harry; although he was lessened at home. His hair was greasy. He was wearing grubby jeans and a knitted pullover with saffron-coloured food spilt on its front. He farted without disguise or apology. She licked up, exalted in such unpleasantness as if it were delightful.

She said, 'I couldn't put the trapdoor back. It was too heavy.'

Brightling said, 'I'll do it. Let's both go up on the roof and let Maud work. What are you drinking, Joan? If we're still friends.'

Joan was rapturously happy. She was on the roof holding a free drink and had been promised a free dinner. She had entered the glamorous world of people with enough to eat.

Beside her, lounging against the parapet, Harry held the bottle and the other glass. He explained how to recognise Georgian wine glasses by the stems.

The grey sky was intermittently radiant. She put up with discomforts such as the cold wind and Harry's bottle-bearing arm which now weighted on her shoulders. She marvelled at his proximate body including the idea of his nakedness and the idea of his each cell's interior hangar crossed by gantries, monorails, floating space junk and speeding messengers. The ecstasy caused by his nearness; and his tainted odours of whisky, digestion, bergamot and the musk of a man neither particularly clean nor particularly unclean; was inseparable from the searing pain of the position he was unthinkingly forcing her into. The musicality of his voice prevented her from understanding his words, which were about monkeys and cats and foxes and pigeons. With fortitude she endured transcendental agony. After what seemed unending discomfort and sublimity there was commotion in the street below.

Tom Shadwell was enthusiastically pointing up at them and oinking and grunting. He thumbed his snub nose. From above his head appeared a block or uneven globe with fibres laid across it. A group of onlookers included two Police Support Officers.

Joan said, 'What's he saying?'

'No idea. Go inside. Talk books to Maud. I'll go down and get him out of trouble.'

Maud explained, 'Tom Shadwell always puts on a show for Harry. He seems to think that Harry is a lord and he is Harry's jester.' She was chopping a swede. 'I am no good cooking out of my own kitchen so I am just doing mashed swede with sour cream, and a salad. I'm trying to get Harry off junk food.'

'I like your breeches.'

'The market, second hand.'

'And your cashmere.'

'My mother, last Christmas.'

The shoes which Maud had kicked off were high heeled. Joan's categorising and tactless mind understood that the shoes which wounded her feet were what Maud must wear to work; the equals of a construction worker's steel-capped boots. She said, 'Are you preggers?'

'Yes.'

'Does Harry know?'

'No.'

Brightling bounded downstairs hastily assembling his qualities as a man of probity. He sucked a peppermint.

Outside, Tom Shadwell had been removed and the onlookers dispersed. He recognised the remaining officer, motherly in her stab-proof vest, who regularly patrolled the market.

He told her, 'Basically I was on the roof to clear the gulley. There's a problem with leaves in autumn. We keep a broom up there. And frankly I enjoyed the view. A thunderstorm would be spectacular, don't you think?'

'Well. This Mr Shadwell. I gather he does odd jobs on the market?'

'Looked after as one of our own.'

'Of course assistants should be properly registered.' She amended kindly, 'No doubt a blind eye is sometimes turned. Does he often cause disturbances?'

'Not often, no.'

'Can you understand what he says?'

'Oh absolutely. Generally. Harder when he gets excited.'

'Do you know his address?'

'No I don't.'

'Do you think he may sleep rough?'

He joked, 'What, on top of a barrow? With the potatoes?'

'But it's possible?'

84

'It's not a question I would ask a free man.'

She consulted her notebook. 'Was there someone with you on the roof?'

'Would you like to speak to her?'

'I don't think it's necessary. We've got enough witnesses.'

'And Tom didn't commit a crime.'

'Other than causing a disturbance. We probably won't do anything more about it. We're more concerned about his welfare.'

Brightling played the part of being without guilt or guile convincingly: he became without guilt or guile. He was cleansed.

'Of course. Is Tom all right? Is there anything I can do?'

'No. It's past our tea time so my colleague has taken him to the café. We've contacted social services.'

Quince-coloured leaves of silver birch blew along the pigeon-coloured pavement.

Joan said, 'He won't be pleased?'

Maud said, 'Probably not.'

'Did he tell you about his red-haired croupier?'

'He mentioned something. But I intend to have the baby. I'm independent. I own my flat, it's in Kew, you must come over. My job is well paid. I can do things. Did you know I plastered and painted the walls at Mostyn and laid the floorboards?'

'Not Harry?'

'Harry delegates. We should get out of your home. Harry always told me how much he likes you and he genuinely believed you preferred the garden flat.' Maud's eyes shone with the frankness and the generosity of the well brought up. 'Rely on me to get all your stuff brought back here. If I were your lawyer I would tell you that this is the more valuable property. I researched an attic extension.

At present we can't get planning permission but the word is the restriction will be lifted. Harry will make money. Although, between us, he's an adventurer with no idea of business.'

'Fuck, is that coat Westwood?'

'Do you want to try it on?'

'Yes. And tell me who are your favourite writers.'

Brightling said, 'I knew the support officer. Nice woman. If anybody wants to be a nice woman. Are you a nice woman, Joan?'

'No.'

'I told her I was going to push you off the roof until Tom's antics prevented me. Do you think I'm joking? Of course I am. Maud is cooking something healthy and vegetarian so I'm off to the Phil U. Isn't anybody drinking?'

Joan Goes Home

Krystina became the tenant of 19 Mostyn Road and in gratitude made the children remove their shoes indoors. Krystina's sister, flautist and office cleaner, shared the flat. Brightling kept away because he did not intend to lose a worker by seducing either Polish woman.

In the dinge-rimmed bath, Joan wrenched hooked molecules of water apart from their mass and threw them at herself.

Harry and Maud had violated her home and although they were gone the avatar of Maud was a yard away, thighs spread on the lavatory seat, reading a book. Harry's avatar lurked naked, silkily and bestially furnished with body hair. His penis was long and slim. The third person was herself at eighteen, during her crush on the original Harry, her unwieldy naïve body thrust into a cotton frock from Wimbledon High Street.

She needed to write but no story could synthesise or reconcile her age with Harry's age. Words put order and control on chaotic experience but she could not control her experience of Harry. Something wonderful had happened on the roof during her unreadiness.

She dressed, picking up her black jumper from where it lay on the floor with its sleeves inside out, and put on the saucepan for coffee. According to her theory, all lovers were Pygmalions and she had created, by bestowing power on a quite commonplace man, the satyr who fucked her dreams.

Her writing life was from one exercise book to the next. As she got older she must race death to finish the work in progress. At the end of the winter when a green speck quickened on the woody stump of last season's mullein; Verbascum Nigrum; she was responsible for the windowbox plants. She speculated against subjective death because only the twice-experienced exists and death, being unremembered, having no rememberer, is experienced once. She also considered that one day she could access her brain and hear white noise. Her brain could break down as had the motor of her fridge which was no longer of use but an assemblage of chubby moulded plastic parts spotted the acid yellow of polar-bear piss on snow.

At least Harry and Maud had given her a free drink and free grub.

A Year Later (More or Less)

It was damp but not windy. Stillness.

In the section of Portobello spanned by the Meccano bridge of the Hammersmith & City Line and the concrete swathe of the Westway most of the traders had left. Only one leisurely loader named Bookman with generator and stereo treated Brightling and anyone else still hanging around to cool sounds.

87

The stalls were metal trestles with a bracket at each corner that held the two H-shaped uprights. At the end of trading, squatters laid out their goods. Brightling suspected that the reward was social because the stuff seemed unsaleable: videos, broken handbags and large drab clothes.

By twilight even the squatters had gone. The air was moist, anticipatory, jazz-bearing, lit by panels on the underside of the Westway. At intervals the reflections of the trains crossing the bridge plunged like fairground dippers in the curved windscreen of a parked van.

Brightling dined from a carton of Curry Chicken. Phil had been retired and the business taken over by his son, also named Philmore. Takeaway customers were given bags but the genius had gone out of the cooking.

The jazz stopped abruptly.

When he noticed Tom Shadwell he realised it must be over a year since their last encounter. Something had happened to Tom. Instead of the filthy anorak, his outfit appeared laundered; but ill-assorted and ill-fitting like clothes issued by an institution. A laminated identity label hung around his neck.

'Tom. How's everything?'

Tom shuffled as if embarrassed by his downgrade from cheerful low intelligence to a medicated condition.

The nearest metal table was covered by a torn sheet. Brightling strolled over and sat on the table. Obediently Tom followed and sat on the table next to it.

Brightling repeated, 'Things are going OK? Have some chicken.'

He had been inebriated on the roof and could not remember whether he had intended to push Joan Byker. He had put Joan out of his mind except that her rent appeared regularly in his bank account. Especially he did not know whether Tom's performance that evening had been on purpose to draw attention to his hero and protect that hero from committing a rash action. There had been no opening to interrogate the market porter whiffing of onions who had in person the infinite rounded surface of a root vegetable and who now grasped a chicken wing in the pudgy fist symptomatic of his condition. The destructive energy of the roof episode had randomly earthed through that integrity, that muddy globular servant. Harry Brightling was not a killer, Joan Byker was alive in her flat, only Tom Shadwell had been captured by Social Services, the 'arsehole' of his irreverence, and now dumbly and bashfully apologised for his unluckiness. His short chubby legs were crossed at the ankles. The felt indoor boots seemed the type that is made in the workshops of institutions for their inmates.

Brightling noticed, under the sheeted table, a box of old hats. He conjured out a joke hat: a fluorescent pink, furry spider. Its glued-on eyes were holograms that shifted perspective. He put on the cartoon hat. Its fluffy legs swayed four each side of his face. Its eyes ogled wildly. He said, 'Things aren't so bad. You've got shelter.'

Tom smiled shyly.

Brightling took off the spider hat, which splashed intense pinkness onto the monochrome dusk, and gave the pink spider and chicken carton to Tom.

Tom beamed. He could tell by the air when the doors closed so quite soon he toddled uphill with his presents to the Sheltered Housing unit attached to the hospital.

A Walk in the Country

The prophylactic against existential dismay being, as mentioned, regular bowel movements and walks, Joan enjoyed outings to London's country. She was in Sussex where she followed a stream that flowed through meadows. A sunny inlet entranced her. She was provisioned with wholemeal biscuits that became pasted to her large teeth in a manner that was not beautiful while her eyes absorbed beauty. The contemplation of sedge grass, particles of mud and green cells suspended in clear water, and fleet minnows, was blissful. Later in the course of her walk she thought analytically that the overflow of spiritual delight, which opposed the catastrophic leakage of spirit that she called dismay, was not the experience of any god or life force. It was subjective, a faculty of spirit as there were physical and mental faculties, and compatible with nihilism. This important philosophical conclusion should not disappoint.

The return towards the railway station was along a winding High Street whose history clearly had segued from track, through bottle glass and bay windows, to plate glass and access through a car park to a chalet-shaped Tesco. She noticed a young woman whose back was crossed by the straps of a baby sling.

Maud turned. To qualify the Madonna look she had razored her hair and painted her nails bright blue. She wore the black Westwood coat over jeans. She said, 'Joan, how wonderful. This is Finn, nine months. We've been along the river. Harry would love to see you. I can't get him out of that gift shop. Let's wait for him in the Gingham café, my treat. Chocky cake.'

Some fifty yards away, Harry presented a mock-up of the urban squire in Harris tweed jacket, fox-patterned cravat, the flaky rock and roll T-shirt, jeans and old Converse plimsolls. He was looking at the shop not at the women.

Joan assented, 'Chocky cake.'

In the café, Maud cradled and adored Finn who slept within the microclimate of infancy. Dark hair wisped from beneath his cap.

Maud said, 'Have you noticed that artists didn't paint Jesus as newborn? Newborns have gluey hair and inflamed skin. The chubby child in the manger is at least six months. He sits unaided.'

When hiking, at two miles Joan's body released the endorphin, the analgesic high that could keep her walking indefinitely. Lately however at five miles her hands became swollen, darkened and numb. Now the old woman poked a blackened finger into Finn's curled fist. By reflex the fist closed around the finger.

She said, 'Ah, the little chap.'

Maud said, 'I was disappointed. I gave you my address hoping you would come round.'

Joan had necessarily denied herself the associative allure of Harry's friends and Harry's woman; renounced the form of obsession by proxy.

Maud continued, 'I have a project while I'm on maternity leave.'

'I like your punk hair. Tell me.'

'Thanks. I cut it myself. I'll cut yours if you like. Well, our world, especially a child's world, includes anthropomorphic animals. In Finn's picture books pigeons wear smocks and foxes wear waistcoats. Finn is too young for observation but my sister's two-year-old has no problem with the dissonance between picture and reality. He is not fazed by animals in clothes. Odder, don't you think, he accepts toy cars and trains with humanoid faces. He doesn't say, "this can't be a train because trains don't have faces". He accepts the hybrid. He also tolerates versions of animals he hasn't seen, such as lions and elephants, and that nobody has seen, such as dinosaurs and by extension cartoon dinosaurs. All these inhibit his world. Do you prefer cappuccino?'

'Yes please.' She noticed that Maud had picked up Harry's winning trick of referral. 'Adults are also accustomed to hybrids. Advertisers draw arms and legs onto packets of the product.'

'My point is that we are specifically receptive almost from birth.'

'Genetically programmed to feel at home among the descendants of animal-headed gods?'

'Exactly. How do you define everything?'

'I would have to think. To be precise. As a random green smear at a fold between quantum physics and astrophysics.'

'So, more or less, do I. Harry sees a theatre, masque or charade. My child enters a world folded not only between microcosm and macrocosm, but with infolds one of which depicts mythical animals and trains with faces.'

Joan said, 'He may grow up to open the fold that sees galaxies of numbers or forests of words. Aren't you having coffee?'

'Not while I'm feeding.'

'Have you and Harry separated?'

'Yes. I'm in Kew and he lives behind a furniture store off Golborne Road. He has a sense of honour whereby he remembers Finn's name and goes out with us occasionally; usually somewhere with an auction house or a junk shop. I've sold the Jag and bought a VW.'

The café's glass door had a gingham flounce. Joan said, 'Will he be long?'

The forecourt of the shop which sold novelties, gifts and souvenirs displayed second-hand domestic goods such as chairs, folded curtains, some children's clothes, a box of picture and photo frames and a tray of cutlery and hair rollers. Brightling guessed that the purveyor of what he and Morgan called 'fucking twee-ware' had, like Morgan, a sideline in house clearances and removals.

One of the frames had its picture still hanging in by two tacks. All afternoon the country had bored him but now he received that unmistakable dealers' or criminals' rush. His ears pricked as the painting informed him of its quality; of how good it was.

The scene had been painted from above; from balcony or first-floor window. A leafy branch in the foreground arced over a group which was disposed in deck chairs in a garden. From the dress the period seemed early 20th century, just before World War One. The central figure, that is the figure whose pose crossed the line whose ratio to the centre most pleases the eye, was slight, bearded and wore a hat. There was a purpose or intention in the selection of the group, as if they were literary or artistic house guests, he thought probably Bloomsbury Group.

The painting was under offer to him for as long as his nonchalant hand rested on it. His body was braced ready to walk away at the slightest inconvenience such as high price. There was a sensation of lightness, of getting away with it, of floating above morality at a level of, amazingly legal, misrule.

When the shopkeeper came out Brightling enquired pleasantly, 'How much for the frame?'

'Don't you want the picture?'

Brightling showed surprise at noticing a picture loosely attached. 'Oh, right, absolutely, if they belong together, I don't mind, yes.'

ACKNOWLEDGEMENTS

'J Krissman in the Park' is published in *The Best British Short Stories 2013,* Salt Publishing

'J Krissman in the Park' and 'Dark Angel' are published online in *3:AM Magazine*

THE AUTHOR

Laura Del-Rivo was born in 1934 into a middle-class family in Cheam, Surrey. She became part of a loose group of writers that included Colin Wilson and Bill Hopkins. Her debut novel *The Furnished Room* was published in 1961. It was hailed by Colin Wilson as 'one of the significant novels of the 1960s'.

In 1963 *The Furnished Room* was turned into a film, *West 11*, by the late Michael Winner. The Furnished Room was republished by Five Leaves Press in 2011. Laura's other novels include Daffodil on the Pavement and more recently *Speedy and Queen Kong*, which was published by Paupers' Press in 2004.

Laura Del-Rivo was photographed by Ida Kar and was featured in the Ida Kar retrospective at the National Portrait Gallery. She lives in Notting Hill and runs a designer tights stall on the famous Portobello Market. Laura has always kept on writing, and all these strands seem to come together in a remarkable short story collection *Where is my Mask of an Honest Man?*

More details are available from
www.hollandparkpress.co.uk/delrivo

Holland Park Press is a unique publishing initiative. It gives contemporary Dutch writers the opportunity to be published in Dutch and English. We also publish new works written in English and translations of classic Dutch novels.

To

- Find out more
- Learn more about Laura Del-Rivo
- Discover other interesting books
- Read fascinating columns in our Anglo-Dutch magazine
- Check out our competitions
- Join the discussions
- Or to just make a comment

Visit www.hollandparkpress.co.uk

Bookshop: http://www.hollandparkpress.co.uk/books.php

Holland Park Press in the social media

http://www.twitter.com/HollandParkPres
http://www.facebook.com/HollandParkPress
http://www.youtube.com/user/HollandParkPress